MW00642057

A CAMERON STONE ACTION THRILLER

STICKS
and
STONES

THOMAS LEBRUN

Copyright Thomas LeBrun 2022. All Rights Reserved.

All rights reserved. This book or any portion thereof may not be reproduced or used in any manner whatsoever without the express written permission of the publisher except for the use of brief quotations in a book review.

Print ISBN: 978-1-66784-769-6 | eBook ISBN: 978-1-66784-770-2

A NOTE FROM THE AUTHOR

To all of you that are involved in the personal security and Martial Arts fields, or just those who want a nice little action adventure to pass the time on a rainy day, I hope you enjoy the book. A special thanks to Dr. Mark Yates of the UK for adding his own little twist to the story. Is this based on a true story? Yes, well except perhaps the parts that are made up.

—Thomas LeBrun

TABLE OF CONTENTS

PROLOGUE

The explosion ripped through the hotel and surrounding buildings bringing chaos to an otherwise crisp, still night air. A thick cloud of smoke spread through the streets as residents gathered outside to watch the fire grow in size and intensity from afar. They seemed unsure if their temporary residences were going to be destroyed in front of their eyes. They feared that the fire and the devastation of the explosion would spread to each hotel in turn. It took with it, without notice, patrons, employees, and innocent civilians out for an evening stroll. The targeted Regency Hotel is located at 61st and Park in New York City.

Along with the extreme pandemonium the explosion caused, the avenue is generally bustling with shoppers during daylight hours and calmer at night. However, on this evening, a Friday night in May 1991, a visiting king from a Middle Eastern country, celebrities from the Broadway and Hollywood sects, and their respective security personnel were all affected as the night was full of dignitaries and a who's who of V.I.P. foot traffic. This night and events would haunt them all for the rest of their lives.

Two of the casualties were a protector's wife, Tessa, and eight-year-old son Michael, the wrong place at the wrong time. They were there to drop off a card at the concierge desk to forward to her husband, best described as a close protection specialist allocated to many High-Net-Worth corporate executives through the years.

The building shuddered violently as though New York City had experienced its first earthquake. The hotel floors rocked up and down like a boat on the ocean, while the walls started to crack. The sound of the blow was loud enough to be heard by the deaf. The explosion brought to life the city's emergency alarms systems, people panicked, and all emotions ran rampant. Then, quickly, reaching for his go bag, weapons, and the like, the agent responsible for the safety of his fortune 500 client responded and reacted, albeit with a touch of adrenaline and controlled fear that dictated his next course of action.

He was racing into the client's room without the heroics of busting the door down; the spare key did come in handy. The client also had pulled the double lock off just as the protector made it to the door. Always a good thing. In protection terms, the client or principal was disorientated based on the manufactured earthquake; he was coherent enough to listen to his guardian. Breaking out a hotel window with a thick bath towel, the agent spied the fire escape that he had located during his initial advance. He had done a perimeter assessment and security advance before the client's arrival. The fire escape was to the left and one story down. With a bit of ingenuity and a bedsheet, the protector lowered himself down first and then guided the client to safety.

After securing and cautiously making their way to the street level, both parties noticed it was anything but secure on Park Avenue. Instead, it looked like a war zone. The first responders and many other emergency vehicles were already on the scene. General panic, screaming, flashing lights, clouds of building dust and debris in the air, looting at a nearby store, and chaotic paranoia seemed to rule the night. The scene was chaos that lasted for several hours as many people were injured or missing. Others were walking around like they were zombies covered in dust. The agent's immediate task was to get the client to a safer environment, as bodies lay in scattered heaps.

In contrast, others who remained alive struggled to get their bearings. It doesn't matter how strong your physical character or stomach is; the heart-wrenching visuals of human despair effects both. This scenery will make you stop dead in your tracks, as did the agent and his protectee. Little did this agent realize that his family members were among the victims of this terrorist event. This heinous act would affect many lives and his for years to come.

The client, at this point, wondered what to do next. He asked the very person, his protector who brought him out of a nightmare to a safer environment, what would be the next course of action. His hands were shaking. The protector had already started to formulate a plan to take stock of what happened, get some sense of bearings, and figuratively collect one's thoughts to move the client to even safer grounds. The agent also reflected that after doing this type of work for an extended time, you get that instinct of whether something is right or something is very wrong. In this case, the latter ruled the day. A phone call home gave him that knot in his stomach when you fear for the worse. Within hours after securing the principal in a nearby hotel with another team member Johnny K., the agent returned to ground zero. He was not sure why; he just did. The dreadful truth revealed by evidence uncovered. The NYPD officer dealing with the aftermath knew the agent and helped him and handed him the card his wife had carried to surprise her husband. It had Agent Raine's name on the front of the blood-stained envelope. While the rescuers recovered his wife's body, his sons dreadfully was not.

Days after the funeral, and sadly, the nightmares began with onset depression and anguish. The funeral was difficult. Burying a family member was something that most people would not want to go through more than once. Yet, now and moving forward, his constant companions seemed to be anger, hopelessness, and poor mental well-being. He was in a fog of depression, living from day to day like a zombie, barely functioning. He was unable to get anything done, unable to think clearly, and with no motivation or drive to change things for the better even if he had the time or inclination to do so.

Edmond Raines, now 38 years old is no longer protecting those who had once needed his expertise by the very nature of their chosen profession, travel concerns, and the like. Now three, five, and ten years had gone by, ten years of trying to escape the gruesome past and the night that shook New York and the United States, for that matter. Ten years of reliving that night and ten years of putting out posters of a boy either missing or having died in the explosion, the exercise ended mainly in dead-ends. Life went on for many after a decade, but time seemed to have stood still for Raines in many ways. Having a hard time rising each morning, drinking, being inactive, working physical manual jobs to stay busy during the day dulled the keen reflexes once honed to a sharp edge but sadly now all in the past. It all seemed so long ago. A no-life attitude added to guilt and depression. Life of a part-time hermit and "Leave me alone" was the conversation of the day. However, a small part of Raines did not entirely give up hope. He obsessively followed up with newspaper clippings for years with friends in the intelligence community concerning the explosion, its aftermath, and any significant discoveries. The investigation had gone on for these last ten years with inconclusive results. There were nearby cameras on during the bombing, and investigators sifted through footage, but the technology was not advanced enough to pick up vital details. Moreover, the explosion seemed to have a snowball effect in 1995 the Oklahoma City bombing; in 1996, TWA 800 exploded off the coast of the northeastern United States into the Atlantic Ocean, and in 1996 a bomb exploded at the Atlanta Olympics.

On September eleventh, 2001, just before nine am on a clear Tuesday morning, an American Airline Boeing 767 loaded with twenty thousand gallons of jet fuel crashed into the north tower of the two World Trade Towers in New York City. Eighteen minutes later, the second tower was hit by United flight 175. Another plane, United flight 93, crashed in Pennsylvania with a target of the Capitol in D.C. Also reported on that flight, the passengers attacked the terrorists forcing the plane to go down. While all this was happening, one more plane, A.A. flight 77, crashed into the Pentagon.

The World Trade Towers event added to other acts of terror; investigators worked tirelessly to find the answers. Unfortunately, for the families whose friends and relatives were victims of these senseless acts, each passing day in their lives with no explanation was too long to wait. This last act of terrorism was too close to home for Raines, and he once again relived that moment a decade ago. He saw his wife and son's faces on videotape on the T.V, but now they were dead and gone. And so were the victims of the attack on the World Trade Center.

Raines missed his former life of protecting people, but much to his surprise, his client of ten years ago stayed in touch for a time, and he, Raines, appreciated it. This former client still used protection wherever he went and used Johnny K. or John Tannon while in N.Y.C. From Raine's professional perspective, there was satisfaction in that his former client was always in good hands and safe.

After all these years of doing investigative forensics, the evidence further came to light that his son was not among the scores of bodies examined as they previously thought to be the case.

Raines tortured himself for not being there, for not protecting his family, and now the uncertainty of what happened to his son. His thoughts brought back memories of his dad many years ago, who worked as a police officer from Brooklyn North.

A Child's Past (Raines)

One night in the middle of a hot summer's evening, there was an armed break-in to the Raines's home in the middle of the night. The burglars had forced their way into the house and were rummaging through the drawers in the kitchen when Mr. Raines woke up to find one of them standing over him with a knife. They threatened to harm his family if Mr. Raines did not follow them downstairs. Edmund's father assured the family that they were safe and had protectively shielded them from the ensuing gunfire that later roared through the house walls when he went downstairs. Edmund's mother covered her son's ears and shielded his body with hers. As a result, both the armed assailant and Raines's father went down, and neither survived.

At the police burial, Raines's father was considered a hero for protecting his family. His father was well-liked and respected by all he associated with, namely his police partners and families in the community. He remembers that night very clearly; he was twelve years old, the year was 1975. It all seemed like a bad dream. Burying his father did not seem real, hoping that one day he would return. He would think of his father every night before bed, and then the next morning, when he awoke, he had to face reality again.

The precinct in which his father worked took outstanding care of young Edmund Raines, professional obligation across the board. The detectives worked with his mother to raise him and taught him right from wrong. They kept him busy with school and extracurricular activities, including a ride-around program with the detectives and often going to the shooting range. This activity was to keep his mind occupied and active, away from the thoughts of the night his dad departed protecting his family. As a result, young Raines knew in his heart; he was being schooled to be a police officer like his dad. Only time would tell. Over the next few years, they dropped him off at Gleason's gym, the most famous boxing gym in Brooklyn, NY, located at 130 Water Street, under the Manhattan Bridge. Although Raines's time there was a period of personal and physical growth, the officers gradually left him on his own and picked him up about three hours later. He came out one day with his nose broken, not crying at all, just a little frustrated that it happened.

Raines became quite adept in the sweet science; the owners were quite impressed with this talented teenager and wanted him to try out for Golden Gloves. He declined and trained obsessively and gladly stood in as a sparring partner for the heavyweights. It got to the point that no one wanted to go up against him in the ring, sparring or otherwise. The detectives themselves shied away from this beast of a young man. They frequently joked about it, but in reality, none of them wanted to be on the receiving end of the young man's developing power. One officer had heard of a small Japanese man that had just arrived in New York City under particular circumstances and would be staying for about six months. His primary goal was training federal agents and local police in takedowns, pressure point control, and joint locks. The detective thought this might just be the person that could train Edmund in very effective hand-to-hand combat techniques. His name was Grand Master Tosh Yokahama. The detectives asked permission to have Edmund train with this master from Japan.

At first, Sensei Yokahama frowned on the idea, still a child, but something about young Raines intrigued him. Raines soaked up everything the Sensei was teaching and picked it up faster than the law enforcement officers who would be on the street day in and day out. There were times that Raines was so focused on learning techniques and was taken in by not only the physical aspects of the arts but also the science behind it. In fact, one day, six hours of training had gone by and only ended because his mother called to see if he was ok.

The Sensei could see that Raines could very well be the prodigy that he sought. Raines was a young man, yet his skills were already second to none. He would not fail to achieve greatness in his future career by either following in his father's footsteps or entering into the private sector doing security for important people in society. It was incredible how he flowed, thought Yokahama, like he's been doing this for a very long time. Raines was a natural, in fact, he was better than most officers.

Furthermore, he noted that Raines's eyes did not lack concentration; instead, they seemed to be on another level with no care of what was happening around him. It's called the three-foot focus. Only when the Sensei said, "Yame," did Raines stop. Sensei Yokahama added more drills to include the wooden dummy of Wing Chun, more bag work, more pressure points, and more of why it all works. He always gave young Raines homework and some advanced techniques that Sensei Yokahama did not think he could master, never mind figured out independently. Sensei Yokahama did that because his time was ending here in the United States, and he wanted this young man to practice as much as possible. Two things bothered Yokahama; first, he would miss young Edmund Raines. Second, he was hoping he would see him again and again to continue the training. The youthful wonder could be someone exceptional in the martial arts world.

The Sensei returned to Japan not before giving Raines his phone number, mailing address, and some motivating words. Through the years, Raines trained like he was on the Olympic team, obsessed with all facets of training. He wanted to get better and better, but more than that, he wanted to prove that he could beat everybody, that he wasn't just a one-hit-wonder. So, he stayed in touch with the Sensei, and the master mailed him a book of intricate movements; the book was called the Tao of Hogoshin-do. The art was for protectors. The translated meaning is "One who protects another with the mind of awareness." Raines thought the book was fascinating. He created a workbook within its pages; one day, he'd ask for another copy with no markings.

One night with friends, Raines and company were eating at IL Mulino's restaurant in Greenwich Village, NY, on 3rd street. A few patrons were getting loud and obnoxious a couple of tables down. The wait staff were unsuccessful in trying to quell the unruly behavior as they tried diplomacy, offering to pay for their beverages but to no avail. The moment they turned around, the behavior would increase and now focus on the employees, sometimes hitting them in the back with bread. Friday night was crowded, and other regulars complained a little, became frustrated, and then left. No one came to take their places until the situation was under control—lost business. Now about nineteen years old, Raines stood up and walked over to the table of loud and obnoxious male donkeys. The table of alcohol and testosterone-fueled men looked up at Raines like they were going to be amused. Instead, Raines looked down and said, "No more."

The loudmouth of the group was about to say something when Raines caught him with a strike at GB20, a pressure point at the base of the skull on either side of the neck. The man was out cold. Raines told the rest to leave and returned to his table. Out of the corner of his eye, he could see the remaining persons of the group pick up their friend and almost tip-toed out. The restaurant was as quiet as a church. Then, one by one, the patrons clapped their hands, and the proprietors came up to Raines, asked who he was and did he need anything in the way of food or drink, and welcomed him to come by any time. His meal was on the house. Raines and his party appreciated the attention, more his party than Raines himself. Kiddingly, but with a serious undertone, the restaurant owner asked Raines if they needed someone like him could they give him a call or how could they get in touch with him? Raines smiled and told him about a signal that could illuminate in the sky but then mentioned he was just kidding as that signal was in use by someone with a cowl. They both laughed. Seriously though, Raines said he would stop by from time to time for some great food.

Raines and friends entered the evening air intending to return to their respective homes when they heard a familiar voice.

"That's him, that's the guy who hit me for no reason in the restaurant." The loudmouth from the establishment had five new friends and a renewed sense of bravado. They surrounded Raines and his friends.

Raines politely requested to leave his friends out of this; the circle parted, leaving Raines one on five odds.

LM shouted with a bit of hesitancy in his voice, "Take him."

Raines executed a spinning hook kick to the jaw of the first attacker, and upon landing, he grabbed the arm of the next attacker and yanked so hard you could hear a distinct pop as the arm hung limp. The third attacker, the biggest, grabbed Raines from behind in a bear hug; without letting him get set, Raines stomped hard on the big man's foot dropped and flipped him into an oncoming bulldozer of a man. The fifth man was about to wet his pants when Raines's fist stopped a hairs width from his nose. After that, Raines told them, at least the ones still conscious not to move.

"Ok," said Raines, "Just you and I. So, you can leave, and we don't talk about this ever again, or?"

Raines extended his hand first; the two young men shook hands more out of respect than anything else. Raines spoke first and asked, "Just curious, we've never introduced ourselves, but can I ask you your name?"

"Yes, of course, my name is John Tannon. And yours?"

"My name is Edmund Raines; people just call me Raines."

Tannon spoke up and said, "Where did you learn all of those moves? Very impressive, and your speed for a big man. Wow!"

Raines told Tannon that he and his friends owed the restaurant a big apology concerning their behavior earlier in the evening.

Tannon's five friends attempted to get up when he told them it might be better if they stayed put for a minute. Meanwhile, Raines's friends stood off to the side and smiled. It seemed like a turning point for a few of them in both groups; not all, but some.

Raines went back to the restaurant and told the owners what just happened and had a feeling that they would not have any more problems from that group moving forward.

Meanwhile, the officers at the precinct where his father once worked were determined to have Raines be part of the law enforcement brotherhood as they were getting ready to sponsor him for the academy. They heard stories of this young man's prowess. They often argued about who would be his field training officer before and after the academy. In the neighborhood, you were either in law enforcement or a fireman. But, much to their surprise and disappointment, Raines turned them down and told them he was going into private security. Luckily for Raines, his reputation from the restaurant incident preceded him. So the word was out that he could take care of issues quickly, without a lot of fanfare. So Raines took up many offers and started to make good money everywhere he went. All details were above board, and the more he was involved and called for special events and various high net worth individuals coming into the city, the more his studies in academia became the focal point in his success. As for physical training, there were times that he made such good money that he treated himself to trips to Japan from time to time to study under Sensei Yokahama and the best students Sensei could find to sharpen the skills of his Gajin.

His Sensei, Tosh Yokahama, was born in 1929. Along the way, he was trained primarily by Morihei Ueshiba, a Japanese martial artist and founder of the martial art of Aikido. In addition, Tosh trained in the martial arts under Mas Oyama, a disciple of Gichin Funakoshi, who he would refer to as his true Karate teacher. Mas was six years older than Tosh, so Tosh had a big brother to train him. Eventually, Tosh moved to China to train in acupuncture and pressure points for healing and defense purposes and fortuitously bumped into Master Ip Man of Wing Chun fame. They trained hard together and became best friends until Ip Man's passing in 1972. After that, Tosh moved to the Philippines for several years to learn Arnis before moving back to his training studio in Japan, located in a small village close to Mount Fuji. He set up his training for all to participate, and his name was soon synonymous with greatness in the arts; great lineage.

Back in Brooklyn

When not on assignment and traveling to Japan, his mother allowed him to build a workout room in their basement complete with weights and bags; otherwise, Raines would often go to Gleason's gym. Consequently, the newbies that did not know Raines volunteered to jump in the ring with him; it didn't end well for many. However, the proprietor was still convinced that Raines could be a champion boxer and wasn't afraid to tell him. Raines would also treat his mother to dinner and spend quality time with her as much as possible; she seemed very lonely and hermit-like. She seemed confused about what her son was doing at times but was very proud of him nonetheless. Then, Raines suddenly went quiet; he had something to tell his mother. She looked at him and asked if he was ok.

Raines broke the ice and said, "Mom, I met someone. I like her and need your blessing. Her name is Tessa."

His mother gave him that smile that all mothers give when they know their children are happy, "Where did you meet?"

Raines told her that it was at one of the restaurants that he and his friends frequented over the last couple of years. He could tell that his mother was thrilled, now to break to her the other news. "Well,

Mom, I very much like her and, well, she has been pregnant for about a month now."

"Does Tessa like you equally? Edmund, you have become a very responsible young man, and I am sure you will do the right thing. When are you due to have the baby?" His mother was calm in her voice and assuming that they had made up their mind.

"The baby will be born just after my twentieth birthday in April, so we have about eight months to get married and settled." Raines was getting excited the more he talked.

"Well, let's get you two married first; well, actually, I'd like to meet this young lady who has grabbed my son's heart so."

The time seemed to fly. Tessa and Raines's mother got along great, and the wedding went without a hitch. It was an intimate affair with only their closest friends and family present as they exchanged vows in front of a small crowd. Then, Tessa's belly grew, and the baby plans began. With the good money that Raines was making in the security world based on regular business opportunities, they bought a house close to his mother as he had the foresight to know he would be out of town from time to time. The baby was born with no complications. They named him Michael after his father.

His friend John Tannon would stop by and visit Tessa and little Michael but mostly watch Raines train and talk about all aspects of his Close Protection tradecraft. At the time, not many were succeeding in the industry. So, it pleased Raines when he found out John Tannon, once a loudmouth and bully, was now a police officer, at least for now, found his calling, it seemed, thought Raines. John himself was very intrigued by Raines's business; he most likely would have decisions to make in the future.

Raines bumped into more people in the Close Protection World along his journey. One notable individual who was a couple of years older than Raines was Mike Evans; it seemed like he knew what he was doing. Mike assumed that Raines had no experience doing anything in the security world because of his age and wanted to show Raines the ropes. Mike was in Special Forces and kept it a mystery. Mike sidestepped the questions but told Raines that big money was made working as private security contractors. "It's all about the money," Mike would often say. He mentioned he was going to go private upon leaving the service. It sounded like he would do it sooner rather than later, thought Raines.

Raines being somewhat naïve at this point in his life, listened to everything he had to say after Mike was discharged from the service. They seemed to hit it off, although Mike appeared to have an edge about him. Mike brought him along on some Close Protection details. All went well. Not knowing Raines's knowledge in the martial arts world, or even the Security/Close Protection business for that matter, Mike attempted to teach Edmund all his favorite moves in self-defense and defense of a third person. Raines pretended to know a little bit without giving his real experience away. Mike got rough on more than a couple of occasions, putting Raines in an assumed problematic joint lock, and asked him to get out of it. Raines tapped out, although he didn't have to. As time went on, Mike seemed very competitive and kind of a know-it-all like he wanted to be Raines's mentor in everything.

On the other hand, Raines studied everything he could on Close Protection work, medical issues that may arise, and some maritime security-based courses. Raines passed them, not always with flying colors; no one said it would be easy. And as well, his physical training kept improving on many levels.

Prologue

Exorcising The Past, The Wheel of Time

Raines needed to get the past out of his head; he needed to think, focus, remember; he wanted a do-over of the past. He wanted to create a new direction; this current one was not working and was very unhealthy.

Raines needed to regain the lost instincts get back to physical training but knew that getting the edge back was not an overnight project. So, for the next five years, he poured his heart into his training. Raines had built a small gym in his home basement for this very reason. But though working out was a good thing, he struggled at times to focus. A bad day of training could turn into a full-blown panic attack if he were to recall the past. Then he'd remind himself of how far he had come and see the faces of his family to resume his training with more vigor and determination.

Fifteen years now had gone by from that fateful moment in 1991, and pulling himself up, Raines went back in his mind's eye. Was there something missing? Being a protector may mean you made enemies along the way. The soul protector and/or a small Close Protection team are the only things between the threat and the person they want to harm, namely your client. When you successfully protect your client, the potential threat may come after your family to divert the focus of the protector; in this case, Raines. How could he have not seen the warning signs if this were the case? Could this all be scattered pieces to a giant puzzle?

Raines decided to start studying world events with a defensive mindset to regain a sense of self. So, he reached out and located a colleague and friend Mike Evans. Mike was someone Raines hadn't talked to in quite a while. Fortunately, Mike was still in the Close Protection world and currently working. Raines wondered if he had any small projects to get him back into the field. So, they had a long talk about Raines's mental and physical well-being, and Mike gave him a few details from time to time. Raines noted that he thought Mike had changed, a bit more hardened and paranoid. So, over the next few years, Raines worked the low-risk, low-level security operations for Mike and appreciated this but knew that perhaps leaving the very environment, namely the city where feeling a sense of tortured emptiness and depression, might be the way to go. But he knew the feeling of being whole again through renewing experiences that would get him back on track, maybe, maybe not.

This plan of a new adventure would take him overseas for a while to train, study, and get his life back. But, if answers to questions of long ago surfaced, he knew he would have to immerse himself totally into the field of protection, reframe his mind but with an added twist; he must now train within the eye of a hunter.

Raines had put a lot of money away over the years, some from an inheritance and a lot from high-risk special security assignments. These funds could last him quite a while for what he had in mind; he could also find other work or find general things to do to keep busy no matter where he lived. So, little by little, Raines closed some bank accounts and paid up his rent in the village for a year at a time. He would send more if need be. The first stop would be Australia.

CHAPTER 1

A KISS IN TIME - PRESENT DAY, MAY 2021

Cameron Stone

Cameron woke to the loud ringing of his phone. He had only just woken, and it took him a moment to realize where he was—in bed, in his house. He lay next to the woman to whom he'd made love to last night after she'd left the party. It was an evening they'd both enjoyed immensely and that had left them feeling relaxed, contented, satisfied, and even closer than before—until the phone rang again, its noise so jarring that Cameron immediately sat up in bed, as though by doing so he could make the ringing stop, or at least reduce its intensity. The ring tone was very annoying coming out of a dead sleep in the wee hours of the morning. It not only woke you but made you want to throw both the phone at a nearby clock across the room. However, it was 2 am, which meant it was an important call, most likely from the West Coast, oblivious to its time on the East Coast.

He hoped it was the former rather than the latter, which dramatically changed his mood.

A whole year or so of the COVID virus had made traveling difficult and prospective clients more or less house-bound. However, the Close Protection Industry was opening up a little. Cam trained and studied subject matter on anti-terrorism to include many of the world's anniversary dates of terrorist activities, maritime security, and its piracy issues, and delved into cybersecurity threats. This obsessive behavior went on non-stop for an entire year to prepare him well for many assignments.

Those in the C.P. business, otherwise known as the Close Protection Business, know that you will always be a student within the industry. But with so much new knowledge being released every month and year, it is never easy to keep up with all the changes and advancements in personal security and protection. Especially when there are so many other things going on in life which take precedence over learning about such matters as safety and security precautions which are taken for people's well-being and comfort while they traveled. There will always be more to learn; studies within academia play a considerable role in one's success, more so than the physical training and what kind of gun you favor. He was also well aware that one could never train too much on physical skill sets, including defensive arts and weapons of all kinds to keep sharp for what-if situations. Cameron knew that hard skills did not make you good at what you did in the business; soft skills and professional presence were the keys. Cameron realized all of the training honed his reactionary drills, protective surveillance drills, and mental conditioning within the protection realm. These disciplines kept him sharp and the ones he would be protecting alive, plus it was great for his mental health and proper mindset.

Upon moving into this big house in Connecticut, Cameron Stone liked that the basement was forty by thirty and had a relatively high ceiling; this was its selling point. He built his fitness studio complete with a power rack with enough weights and bars to have multiple trainees. Cameron arranged his Wing Chun dummy, a two-hundred-pound heavy bag, and a speed bag in strategic places. Leaning up against the far wall were two big tires, seven hundred and fifty and nine hundred pounders.

With all the training he had been involved with lately, perhaps a new security detail was what was on Cam's mind while he was sleeping, then the phone had rung.

She lay by his side; she, too, heard the annoying ring tone and knew the drill. He would shower to wake up, take out a folder or make a new one specific to the case, turn on his computer, put on some coffee, and prepare some fast food, although it looked like a buffet at times. All this was followed by making endless calls to available agents, airports, car services, and law enforcement agencies, all of the above if needed, and out the door running in three to four hours if the urgency was great enough. She worried about him every time he went out with every what-if situation, more negative than positive; she was in love; what could she say. However, much to his credit, he stayed in touch as much as possible when on an assignment. The communication was romantic and appreciated. She loved it; it had a dual meaning and was understood and noted. It was not the first time that she felt that way, but it did have a special meaning for her because of the feelings of love and affection that he expressed through his words and gestures in all his conversation, that lasted about ten minutes only. While the distance separated them, they often talked about more personal things to make each other smile more than anything else. The phone calls were his brief escape from the daily stress of protecting the rich and famous and sometimes the not-so-famous. Selfishly, she missed him when he was away and also during some of his intense, borderline obsessive solo three-hour training sessions that kept him ahead of the curve. Sara, short for Saratova, missed Cam's warm body and the sense of security and humor he brought into the home and relationship. She rolled out of bed and slipped into something that was very much the flavor of Victoria's Secret. How ironic, as the slinky lace kind of bedroom accessory that did not cover many secrets hung revealingly onto her very athletic body. She teasingly wanted to give him the most revealing of visuals if he was to leave sooner than later. But, of course, she had hoped for later. The outfit would certainly be an invitation to a definite bedroom lullaby.

Sara smiled secretly at all the intimate possibilities. She felt very comfortable in her blond hair, blue-eyed, five-foot-nine, and exceptionally supple frame, like the female athlete Valerie A. to compete in track and field for the United States.

She had attained physical prowess through continuous training by vigorous exercise, swimming, dancing, and running. Unbeknownst to Cameron, she was also an expert in practicing Parkour (free-running) and a very accomplished master of Martial Arts of various disciplines. A girl has to have her secrets. Her doctor recently told her that thirty minutes of exercise each day would be very beneficial; apparently, her doctor had not checked her present conditioning very closely. Her physique would have told the whole story. But what the heck, she thought thirty minutes of vigorous exercise would keep her heart rate up, just the way the Dr. ordered; well, maybe not quite, but it had promise with Cam helping. She helped Cam pack and slipped a pair of her black thong underwear scented with diamond perfume in his luggage. Oh, how she liked teasing him and could imagine seeing his face upon discovery of her unmentionables. Or better yet, one of his teammates and the explanation afterward.

She watched him stretch from the bedroom as he loosened up his muscles. She had to hold herself back from attacking him with loving obsession as she felt droplets of sweat cascade down her spine onto her backside. He had nothing on but Mr. Coffee, her lips moistened with romantic anticipation. Cameron Stone stood six feet, two inches tall, two hundred and twenty-five pounds, muscular, very strong, but very limber like a human leopard of sorts. Sara was in a dream-like state when it became apparent that Cam was looking at her with passion-filled eyes. Her heart pounded as she recognized the unmistakable signs of desire radiating from him like heat off a furnace, and her knees grew weak from the intensity of his lustful stare. Their eyes locked, and she knew their foreseeable time spent in bed was either going to be a marathon of hours or an intense thirty minutes of lovemaking. Either way seemed just fine with both parties.

It wasn't long ago; she thought, when he gave her that first deep open mouth, Hollywood-type kiss. She told him that never had she been kissed like that before. He was quick to reply that the memory made his heart skip a beat, and it too was a first for him. Affectionately she whispered she could see his nose growing.

As the passion began its ebb and flow, both parties knew that it would never be enough, no matter how many minutes or hours went by. Love seems to make the concept of time go away until you are out of time. Unfortunately for them, the lovemaking came to an end, and he silently, like a big cat, rose for the inevitable, his departure. The detail was going to take place in N.Y.C. He slipped on some jeans, a black polo shirt, and a light jacket, grabbed his luggage like it was weightless, put it by the door, and came back to the bedroom, embracing tears and silence from her lips. She slowly stood sans Victoria's Secret negligée. She gave him one of those I love you, and I miss you, I need you kisses look. He returned it in kind with his deepness enveloping her lips. He wiped the tears from her eyes, brushed the blonde hair from her face, and whispered he would be back soon. She knew he would; she could count on him with her heart. She had heard these words before, but a veil of darkness, just for a brief moment, passed by her sub-consciousness. He left a short time later; the client, a Fortune 500 businessman, needed the best. Sara crawled back in bed and enjoyed the smell of the last moments of passion they spent together.

Sara drifted off into a deep sleep. Cam was always on her mind. Living on the edge, in a dangerous business with his head constantly on the swivel, Cam knew his tradecraft. Within the C.P. business, taking the bullet for someone else had to be the most unselfish occupation in the world. Sara had this thought in her mind. She saw Cam in her dream-like state, discreetly looking one way then another, dissecting and scrutinizing the smallest of details, threat or otherwise. Sara saw him walking with his client in her dream, eyes scanning for unusual movements, sudden movements, hands: always the hands, all the while pretending not to be working. The attack she knew could come from anyone anywhere: male, female, short, tall, any race, any weapon. And then it happened she saw a petite non-descript person, could not tell if it was a male or female, age thirty-five to forty-five, pulling out a gun. It all happened in slow motion. Cam was the first target; the gun fired twice. Sara awoke sweating, wondering if it was a premonition of things yet to come; it was surreal.

Now that she could no longer sleep, she donned her sweat suit and went outside to another fitness area. It was complete with various gymnastic equipment, more tires, and four by six-inch beams from tree to tree. It looked like a workout area used on the American Ninja program. Their workout, when Cam was home, included Arnis or stick-fighting. Back and forth, they went with the escrima sticks. The flow was great, and the speed was hypnotic. Sara and Cameron liked competing against one another, whether with the escrima sticks or the challenging obstacle course. Inwardly Sara smiled as she most often let him win as she could do most of the program with her eyes closed chiefly based on her training in Parkour; well, maybe except for the tires, he owned that one. Today's training would go about 2 hours, with the house's roof added to the course. Sara enjoyed this type of workout. It made her feel alive, like when she first picked up the sport of Parkour or free running. She gave Cam credit, though as he did the entire training sessions with a weighted vest on sometimes a thirty pounder, sometimes a fifty.

CHAPTER 2

SARA

Sara was born Saratova Mikova in Prague, the Czech Republic, in 1983, not far from the Shadow Bridge. Her parents lived in Prague when the Russians invaded the city in 1968. On August 20, 1968, about 200,000 troops and 5,000 tanks invaded Czechoslovakia.

When Sara was ten, the family moved to Paris. Her parents put her in the best of schools and wanted her to study ballet, as they were opera and ballet enthusiasts. She appeased them and was quite good but also wanted to play with her friends, and thus the parkour training and martial arts began. Parkour was like training in a giant playground. It was an exhilarating, dangerous sport that took place on rooftops and around trees, in abandoned buildings, under bridges and on the ground among the city's most treasured monuments, all of which were off-limits to Sara and her friends at that time. Her parents, intrigued, saw the poster describing what Parkour was. They found the following:

"Parkour's sport or exercise is by overcoming obstacles in ordinary street settings, and some manufactured some perhaps not and urban environments. The training is like gymnastics over alleyways and the tops of buildings and other barriers through natural movements and various techniques such as jumping, vaulting, flipping, and balancing. The principal idea is to become strong both physically and mentally."

Perhaps a bit on the daring, crazy side, her parents quickly deduced, but she looked happy leaping around on her giant community playground.

Sara and her friends were the talk of the city as people on the street would admire the acrobatic nature of the sport going from building to building effortlessly. The street folk would drop money in a plastic bank to see more. The dancing made her graceful; the martial arts made her street-tough and gave her confidence. She seemed to pick up everything relatively fast. Her martial arts training combined Savate, Judo, Arnis to include bladed weapons and a taste of Krav Maga into a deadly combination.

As she grew older, young Sara became a formidable athlete. She was competitive and worked tirelessly day and night to improve her stamina and strength. But she was very much under the radar as she blossomed in many ways into her twenties, during which she pursued her teaching degree.

Like a curious cat, there were countless times when she heard the police sirens. She would hop onto a roof and practice her free running from rooftop to rooftop to a possible robbery or assault and personally have things taken care of before the police arrived at the scene. She found it exhilarating and lots of fun, dangerous but fun. There were times when shots rang out in her direction, but only once did the projectiles nick her. Sara did not want to come across as a cat woman-type hero but just someone who could help proactively. She would arrive, take care of business, get to the person who was being assaulted, get them out of harm's way, and make the attacker wish for a different ending. In the case of robbery, Sara would typically get a little more physical and test her martial prowess. She would physically retrieve and return stolen property to its rightful owners and leave without being identified. Her oversized hooded sweatshirt hid her blonde hair and feminine curves and even disguised the fact that there might even be a man underneath it all. It wasn't until Sara was twenty-eight that the authorities had their suspicions and surmised who this individual could be, trying to be more than a Good Samaritan. It was funny when many of her parkour friends dressed like her, hooded sweatshirt and all, and went in different directions to throw the police off slightly. But, to no avail for some reason, it just didn't work; the police must have had her under surveillance for some time to be that confident and convinced it was her.

The Chief of Police, Mr. Henri Phillipe-Brun, visited her parents and suggested that perhaps it was time for their daughter to move out of Paris. He said she should consider going to America and start a new life. This proposal made after a long, constructive one-sided conversation was the right decision.

Although they appreciated her help, they genuinely feared for her safety. They did not want a vigilante-type running around in their city. It was just a suggestion, a relatively strong suggestion with no wiggle room. So, she went off to America and legally changed her name to Mitchell, Sara Mitchell. America, the land of opportunity.

Much to her surprise and a little pre-investigation before leaving Paris, she found a small town named Westport, Connecticut, that looked like it had promise. Next, she found a small, affordable, single dwelling home and neighbors, very nice people who were far enough away for personal privacy. Also, the city had an excellent school system where she applied and secured a position teaching French to fourth graders. Finally, her parents had given her enough money to buy a car, settle in and create her own new life. Sara continued her exercise regimen, which now included swimming. She found a Martial Arts Center nearby, specializing in Boxing, M.M.A., self-defense, and the like. Her previous self-defense training came in handy as some locals wanted to test her skills at the facility and were aptly embarrassed.

Through the years, Sara explored the city, its pulse, and local eateries. One day, she noticed that her favorite restaurant, The Spotted Horse Tavern, seemed quite busy with patrons. Was there a holiday coming up? She went in and decided to eat at the bar, didn't have a choice, no problem there. The salads and burgers looked great. Sara was taking everything in when in walked this well-built dark-haired, blue-eyed athlete of a man.

"Anyone sitting here?" Sara either did not hear him, or the sweat and flush she felt upon hearing his voice made her oblivious to the question. "Hi," he said, "My name is Cameron. May I sit here?"

Bonjour, je m'appelle Sara. Est-ce que tu habites dans le coin? Vous venez souvent ici?

"Oh, sorry, my name is Sara; I'm sure you don't speak French. I wanted to know if you came in here often." Purposefully, Sara omitted the part when she asked if he lived in the area.

After ordering, Cam told her that he'd been away for some time on business trips and came back from time to time.

Sara told him that she was a teacher and had been here for a couple of years now and when asked what he did, he seemed to be evasive. Finally, it came out that he did security work. Like many, she wondered if he was like a bodyguard like a movie of the same name. She smiled, and Cam could have sworn that her eyes went from blue to green and back in an instant.

So teasingly, now she was having fun and asked him, "So if I attacked you, you could put me down, and there would be nothing I could do."

Cam composed himself and indicated that if someone were to attack her, he would have to defend her honor, kind of side-stepping her question.

The tavern owner broke the moment and told them that their food was getting cold. He also had turned the television on and onto a local station. The scene was three men questioned by the police; it looked like they were in a lot of pain. As the story unfolded on the news, the three men were trying to mug someone coming down a nearby unlit street. Unfortunately, their potential victim was much more skilled than they were, albeit with baseball bats.

As the first attacker came at the potential victim, bat held high, a front kick landed under his chin, knocking him out—the two remaining attackers charged simultaneously. One of the attackers caught the victim's shoulder with the bat but paid for it with an elbow strike to the jaw. The final attacker paused for just a moment, and his reward was a stomp kick to the ankle and a low roundhouse inside of the knee. Finally, the intended victim took one of the attackers' phones, dialed 911, gave the police an idea of what happened, and left the scene. The police chuckled at this last statement of one man taking on three and then called the nearest officer to investigate.

During the police interview, the live news crew caught some of the actual conversations of the assailants.

It seems that once the first assailant took the kick in the jaw, he was out until the police arrived. However, the broken jaw of the second assailant prevented him from articulating some words, so his words were garbled and unclear, and the third person interviewed had a fractured leg. The police asked for a description of the person who did this damage. However, it still wasn't clear if one person, very skilled or multiple people, had thwarted their attack.

Sara wondered naively if this happened sporadically around here. Was it something she had been unaware of for the last couple of years? But, on the other hand, perhaps she thought this handsome man to her right would be so kind as to walk her home tonight. Win-win for everyone.

Cam, reading her mind, said if she felt safer, he would walk her home. No sense leaving her unprotected. Sara reacted teasingly by hitting him in the shoulder and saying something like I can handle myself; perhaps it's you who needs my protection. Then, as she turned her head just for a moment, Cam winced from her blow to his upper arm. The walk home to Sara's place was uneventful, just taking in the crisp night air with Sara breaking the silence by asking if he would be staying put for a while. She said she would like to get to know him more personally. Damn, there go those green eyes again, Cam smiled.

CHAPTER 3

RAINES 2010

Raines thanked Mike Evans for the Close Protection details, but something was missing and something he felt he needed to do. His funds would last for quite some time for what he was planning long term. Raines thought to go to various countries, starting with Australia, getting the necessary visa requirements together; Raines could stay for twelve months. Then, he would apply for visas in other countries as time went by. All this he did not share with anyone, including Mike.

After a few layovers, crossing the international dateline, he ended up in Melbourne, Australia. The taxi driver brought him to the harbor; he surmised Victoria Harbour. First, he looked for a houseboat for sale and a place to doc the boat. Raines found a fifty-foot vessel with all the comforts of home. The boat, Raines noted, had all relatively new modern appliances, an electric stove, a refrigerator and even a hot water heater for a shower. The shower would feel good after a long workout and help wash the salt and grime off after a dip in the ocean. It even had a queen-sized bed that welcomed change from sleeping on the hard ground or metal bench which seemed like light years ago. No one could say that he didn't know how to enjoy himself in paradise at least while it lasted. He also found that many of the boat's mechanical things such as the motor and navigation system were new. It was seaworthy and after haggling with the proprietor they settled on a purchase price of two-hundred thousand dollars with six months' rent upfront for a spot on the dock. Next on the list was transportation. He found that perhaps just a ten-speed road bike would do the trick for now. That way he could go out and get himself some groceries in town, maybe even stop at one of the local restaurants, which were all within walking distance from the dock.

Fighting jet lag, he noticed seafood restaurants numerous in and around the harbor. But, in reality, Raines's heart was set on a place to work out, primarily a boxing or M.M.A. facility where he could start to get himself back in shape. He found a couple of them that looked promising. One that Raines was going to check out was Extreme M.M.A. He discovered that this establishment was not too far from his location. So, he went there, bringing a small gym bag, an extra T-shirt, an old mouth guard, worn-out gloves from yesteryear, an old school eight-track player with tunes, and some sneakers. Upon entering, he knew right off he was in the right place. An octagon cage in the center and serious contenders and other onlookers stopped and looked at Raines. Wrinkled clothes, unshaven, graying hair, he looked like an out-of-shape homeless person who just happened to walk in off the street.

The manager asked, "Something I can do for you, mate?"

Raines just shrugged his shoulders and said he just wanted to work out and asked how much a six-month membership would cost.

"Ah, an American!" the manager said in a loud voice. It got everyone's attention. "I suppose you want to get right in the ring. May I suggest that you get in shape first; then, if you are man enough, we can talk about giving it a go with one of my mates here."

Raines shrugged again and asked what bag he could pound on for a while. The manager pointed in a general direction where the bags hung. Then, he spied one in the corner, looked to be about one hundred and fifty pounds. This bag will do, he thought out loud.

The manager took Raines' money and said, "Have at it, don't hurt yourself." He also thought this might be interesting to watch at least for one round, which he felt would be it.

Raines found a jump rope and started his warm-up. Five minutes later, he squared off against the bag. Putting in the earbuds, he started with Guns and Roses. Raines looked at a nearby timer, and the curious onlookers snickered.

Round after round went on with this stranger in their midst. Raines did forty pushups between the five minutes of timed boxing rounds and other techniques, changed his music to ACDC, Motley Crew, Def Leopard, and began again. This workout went on for ten rounds, striking the bag at a reasonably hard pace. Finally, drenched, he told the manager that he would see him tomorrow same time. There was not a peep from the staff or others in the gym.

Raines went outside and almost puked from exhaustion. However, he did not want to give the M.M.A. crew a reason to think less of him. Riding back to the boat, Raines knew that it would be a long road ahead, no excuses in training. He would just have to get better at everything he did, faster and stronger and more effective inside and outside the gym. Taking a shower on his boat and drinking two liters of water, he pulled his hair back and headed to the first seafood place he could find. Train, rest, and eat fish, what a life.

He found the salmon and vegetables to be a great way to end his day, and tomorrow he would find a breakfast place and carb up for training. Then, thinking out loud, he wondered if the locals had a preference for an excellent place to fish as he had a freezer on the boat.

The next morning, he found himself in front of the mirror, getting ready for training and wondering if there were any new changes to his routine this time around. Week after week, training seven days per week, Raines's schedule did not change just his weight; it went down about twenty pounds to start. The fish and veggie diet agreed with him.

The patrons noticed Raines's training discipline at the facility and asked if he were training for something. Raines's answer was, "Life." They seemed to pause every time he walked in to see how long he would go and anything else he was going to throw at the bag. Curiously, one day they noticed him with a steel bar, rubbing it up and down his shin, apparently numbing the nerves. The next day he did shin kicks; it looked like he had some Muay Thai training or similar hybrid art. Finally, Raines asked one of the M.M.A. athletes to hold the bag while he kicked it. "Sure," replied an athlete. Then, Raines let loose a right shin kick, and the one-hundred-and-fifty-pound training bag almost folded in half, or so it seemed to the fighter holding onto it.

"Damn," said the athlete. "Where did that come from?"

Everyone stopped, and one participant whispered, "I think he's been playing with us all along." While another spoke up and said, "I still don't think he's that tough."

Later, while traveling back to his houseboat from the M.M.A. facility, his travel route became blocked by two of the M.M.A. patrons from the gym.

"Hey Mate," one of them said, "You've hit the bag every day for a few months, done your exercises but never once stepped in the ring. Anyone can hit a bag! Bags don't hit back, mate."

Raines got off his bike, arms loosely to his side, looked at two of them, and said, "Ok."

The smaller rushed in, and Raines shin kicked him hard on the left thigh connecting with a pressure point, in the meridian world; it would be Gall Bladder 31. This point would feel like a Charlie horse, only Raines kicked him with medium power, and to the potential bully, it felt like his leg had broken. The larger one with the big mouth, who was very skilled and surprisingly fast, connected Raines's nose with a powerful left jab. He followed up with a powerful right cross which Raines anticipated, and lowered his head. The right fist connected with Raines's forehead, and a cracking noise sounded. It seems like Raines's head was more rigid than the bare and now broken knuckles from the tough-guy wanna-be. Raines slipped to his right and poked him firmly in Spleen 21, upper outside ribcage. That point always smarts, this time more so than just a little. The pressure point is located on the ribs. The exact location is on the adjacent aspect of the chest, in the 6th inter-costal space. An intercostal space is a tissue between the ribs and centers for nerves. Raines snapped his previously multi-broken nose back in place, which unfortunately happened numerous times over the years. He then looked at his gym buddies, got back on his bike, and headed back to his houseboat, a little upset that he got hit at all. A couple of Advil and some ice would do the trick. He felt a little bad for the two from the gym, well maybe not that bad, slight grin.

The following day Raines was back in the M.M.A. facility sport-ing a pair of raccoon eyes from the broken nose. The manager smartly commented, "What happened to you? I'd hate to see the other guy."

Raines replied that he had a bike accident. "The bike is doing fine, thank you for asking."

With that, Raines went through his workout and started to kick the bag in every way he seriously could muster. Finally, a jumping side kick sent the bag on its journey, and Raines let loose a right punch that stopped it dead in its return. This intense workout went like this for eight more rounds. To conclude, Raines ended his day at the facility, went back to the boat, and grabbed the owner of the boat rental com-pany, and they both went fishing.

After catching tuna, shark, mackerel, salmon, and the like, enough for Raines's freezer and some for his landlord, the landlord asked Raines what he thought of the terrorist buzz on the Internet lately. Raines forgot all about the Internet, and that mobile phones seem to be the rage. The boat proprietor, let's call him Mick, said yes, technology would soon take over, but you would be hard-pressed to find a great signal. So, Raines thought for a minute and asked what it would take to get a good internet signal. The reply was a better tower. So, Raines suggested that they lobby with the other boat owners and neighbors and get a better internet/Wi-Fi tower. The locals were very interested in a petition. They had the where-with-all to get the cell tower that many wanted within no time. The funds came in generously from many, and Raines was their savior within weeks. The cell tower was a reality. In return, Raines indicated that he would be taking off for a little while and asked if he would please hold his docking space. Hopefully, he will be back in six to nine months. Little did Raines know it would be years before he returned.

His next stop would be Bangkok, Thailand, and maybe he would get a long-term stay up to six months before moving on. Once Raines got there, he sought out the oldest, most serious training facility available, the Petchy Academy, or something similar to that, a well-known and one of the oldest Muay Thai Box camps globally.

CHAPTER 4

CAMERON - NYC 5/21

It was a pleasant spring day in May; the air was cool and a little crisp at times, but a gorgeous day nonetheless. The sky was mostly clear, with only scattered clouds to be seen, and it gave a wonderful blue tint to the sun, which had just reached its peak above the horizon. Cameron and two other agents were finishing up protective advances to hotels and restaurants, the latter of which the High-Net-Worth client had wanted to eat at during his visit. The team ran the routes and traffic concerns during the morning, lunch, and five o'clock traffic hours. What streets were under construction? And most importantly, how had Covid changed the way people traveled? These are basic things that were always on the checklist if you will. Were there any dead areas for cell service?

Cam always carried two phones. Was the Waze app on the mobile device accurate in the concrete jungle? Before the client came in, the airport was the last part of the advance. He would be traveling by private jet and landing in Teterboro, New Jersey, from the West Coast and landing about noontime. Cam and the team would plan on getting there about 10 am. A private jet with G-five power could catch a tailwind and cut some time off the projected landing time. It happens.

The West Coast office would give us wheels up. They called, and one of the first questions asked by Cam was if the client was traveling alone. Cam called him Mr. Mike, mostly because he couldn't pronounce his last name. The client liked that, better than saying Sir all the time.

The call came through, and Cam's question was answered; he was not alone, and his spouse would be accompanying him on this trip. Cam asked if there was anything else he needed to know. Unfortunately, the secretary had no other info available.

The jet landed at eleven o'clock, one hour ahead of schedule; all was good. Cameron greeted the client and led him to the vehicles. There were two agents in the tail car, Cam and the principal and spouse in the lead, and another two on standby. Some small talk but otherwise a quiet ride into New York City. Everyone was staying at The St. Regis Hotel, where security was top-notch, and the concierge department never ceased to impress Cam and/or his clients.

After introductions, Cam scheduled a meeting with the clients regarding meetings, dinners, and the like. He informed them that the reservations are confirmed in all locations involving food.

The week went by without a hitch. Pre-advance, protective awareness, and adaptability to any changes in the itinerary were the tools and the norm. Only once did the team flinch as a car backfired, which made a noise similar to a firearm discharging. All scheduled meetings in the city seemed to go very well. As well, the client's spouse went off to shop with one of the team members as her security—no incidents to report on the side trip. Lastly, heading to the airport, the client expressed his pleasure to Cameron in making the trip safe and enjoyable and mentioned he would be traveling again soon.

If the project is successful, there would be nothing to report, but Cam always did an after-action report to see what his team did right and what could be improved. So, Cam called the West Coast, informed them of wheels up, and waited another thirty minutes; now, the assignment was complete. But out of the blue, a production manager that Cam knew called him to see if he was busy as he had an artist named RJ coming into the city for a premier. Cam answered in the affirmative and relayed that a team of three Close Protection agents, including himself, were already in place. Cam also called Sara and told her he would be in the field for a few more days, a red-carpet affair. "Great," said the voice on the other end, sounding sad. The production manager gave all the particulars. The hotel was the Four Seasons Hotel, and the event itself would be at Broadway Theater 1681 Broadway.

However, in his information gathering, Cameron noted that the client they would protect made controversial statements previously covered by a news program that may prompt tighter than usual coverage.

As indicated, the movie premiere was music-related, so the team needed to know that Cameron's appeal to get more protection specialists was not currently in the plan or budget.

"Not going to happen," said the production manager. The client wanted to move about freely without too much security. So, Cam also briefed the drivers, who were the two that were on standby from the last detail.

Before the client's arrival, they went over the protection plan with venue security and the production staff. They also set up a communication or command center with codes and frequencies for all security and production staff in case of emergencies as they each carried one if not two radios.

All security did a walkthrough, and Cameron came up with a question about the recent negative media press. The publicity person handling the event told him that it was nothing to be concerned about; famous last words. Barricades, some wooden, some metal, lined both sides of the red carpet. The crowd would include autograph seekers, press, and curious onlookers. The team's vehicles would be mobile, close to the red carpet. Cam also had a car at the theater's back for emergency evacuation once the party was inside. The production manager indicated that the client/artist would arrive at the theater shortly and to look for a white stretch limo. Cam asked what company was driving the limo and the license plate number as there would be many limousines pulling up and dropping off. People looked dumbfounded by this question, but that prompted a few people to get on the phone and ask questions. Cam and the team checked communications and all seemed to be working fine.

The limo pulled up, and they determined that this was the client; Cam checked the number place that the team received seconds ago, all was good so far. The client got out and spotted Cam and immediately told him where to stand. Cameron gave him a very, shall we say, professional look, which ended the conversation. Cam had one team member near the end of the red carpet watching Cam's six, or back for civilian types. The other team member was in the back and to his right, but he was looking for Persons of Interest. Everyone was mobile.

As expected, someone yelled about the artist's negative political statement that had been previously broadcast in the news and on many social media platforms. This created a frenzy, which instigated more yelling and negative publicity. With cameras rolling, the barricades seemed to be at a breaking point. Cam shouted in his mic, 'Evac now.' Cam put his hand on the client's arms just as the first barricade gave way, trampling people. The screams were piercing. The client looked panicky, and Cam told him they had him covered. Dan, Cam's teammate, helped Cam spin, cover, and evacuate the client towards the waiting cars about sixty feet away. The second barricade gave way, and total pandemonium broke out. Cam, separated from the client because of the sheer numbers of the crowd and also recognized that Dan and Phil had the client.

Cam yelled into his mic, "Get out, get out; I will catch up." He also noticed cameras were rolling with or without handlers. Of course, people, in general, were getting footage on their mobile devices.

In ultra-slow motion, Cam saw the glint of steel in more than one hand. The attackers were bent on inflicting pain on someone, and it just happened that they spotted Cam. Cameron thought briefly that this was not like the movies where the hero comes out uninjured during a violent altercation scene after scene. They charged at him together, kind of like a sandwich, Cam in the middle and their hands held low. It was like they had done this before. It wasn't just one jab with the knife; it was constant thrusts like doing multiple jabs with an edged weapon. Cam parried, evaded, and applied his offensive damage. This street violence was real-world and worst-case.

As crowded as it was, Cam sent a well-placed spinning back kick into the nearest attacker's leg, stopping him solidly as he felt the assailant's knee give out, bending and breaking grotesquely, and spun to face the next assailant. Then, he felt yet another person grabbing him from behind, which prompted Cam to strike with all his might with his elbow; he heard a few ribs crack. He then felt multiple hard punches, a strange feeling to his liver area; this made Cameron take an intense breath. At the same time, the first attacker's knife sliced across Cameron's chest.

CHAPTER 5

HELPLESS

Sara received Cameron's text message and knew it was part of the industry. She knew he would be home soon, safe and sound. But she was daydreaming about Cam again and decided to turn on the TV.

Breaking news; Live; The Artist RJ was on the red carpet when all pandemonium broke loose. The barricades broke loose and collapsed because of spectators, press, curious and obsessed onlookers; the barriers bent and splintered under their sheer weight and collapsed. Many people trampled, and some were seriously injured, if not dead. The TV showed images of cameras left on the ground but kept rolling with disastrous footage. Security on site was limited to some in-house personnel and the protection team provided to the artist.

Sara had put on her DVR when she first heard about an incident in NYC. She would show Cameron when she reunited with him in a couple of days. Sara watched as the panicked crowd consumed the artist only to see him emerge on the other side with two security individuals and vehicles at the ready. She wondered what detail Cam was on. Sara went back into her messages, and he did mention being on a red-carpet affair. Then she saw him, although at a weird angle, trying to fight his way out of the crowd. People were attacking him. She couldn't tell who was hitting him and who was pulling him down on top of other people—and then he fell forward with an awful thump onto the pavement. She saw the knives and splintered wood implements in the hands of attackers and saw him fighting back; then, the mob kicked the camera out of range. It made her jump when a gunshot rang out, Sara felt helpless.

CHAPTER 6

TRAINING FOR LIFE

Raines found the Petchy Academy reasonably quickly and even found an apartment near the training facility. The training here was severe, just the place he wanted to be, in that now he wanted to join in with the best. The younger students were not a threat. They could not get past Raines's strength as an athlete during sparring sessions, so Raines didn't worry so much about them as competition. What and who he did worry about were the senior students and instructors, on a whole different level, and they put him in his place reasonably quickly. Raines ran every day and practiced hand and leg techniques. Since he was the giant American, asking him to get in the ring was a given. But, this time, differently than his Australian trip, Raines said sure.

He outweighed the most prominent of athletes there by about forty pounds. His opponent gave prayers around the ring, and Raines did not know the tradition and bowed deeply. Then, they squared off, and Raines's opponent leaped into the air for a flying elbow technique that was supposed to land atop Raines's head. He missed, but barely. Next, he shot a front thrust kick, hitting Raines in the stomach. Wow!! Raines thought a great deal of power for one not as large as he. Then the kicks were coming in fast succession to his thighs. Damn, he felt as though his leg was damaged, if not broken. Lastly, a high, swift round kick got Raines' attention, brushing his face with power and speed behind it. Raines thought sarcastically; his opponent took it easy on him and later found out he did. Now it was time to train in this deadly art of Muay Thai. Raines knew he would be here for at least ninety days and perhaps get an extension. He was now getting extremely focused as he had been many years ago. The training was going to be his way of life seven days a week, twice a day. Waking up in the middle of the night and spending the whole night doing push-ups or sit-ups had become a habit; he needed to stay fit for the next day.

He got in the ring more often and applied new techniques and grit. Lately, the other athletes seem to bow much deeper; maybe it was the respect that he did not give up easily, or perhaps they felt sorry that he had to take so much punishment. Running, jumping rope, pad work in the ring over and over round after round became habitual. He may have climbed to the third ring of a ten-ring ladder by the second month. The only advantage was his previous training in Australia, whereby he wasn't a fish out of the water by any means showing up in this environment. His endurance was getting even better with each passing day, down another ten pounds. Plus, as the athletes found, Raines had heart, he had the motivation, and he wanted the training in all facets to be as hard as they could muster. Raines believed he got their attention as they hired a masseuse to un-knot his muscles. By the end of the third month, he decided it was time to head elsewhere; the training team gave him a send-off and opened arms should he ever want to return.

The next stop was the Philippines, where Raines wanted to re-study Arnis/Kali and whatever else was happening. Outside of Manila, there, literally in the woods, was a training camp. He knew someone who could make an introduction. It was at the School of Arnis that Raines settled on. They had everything going on, sticks were clicking, and onlookers were mesmerized by the speed and power of all athletes. All athletes were reaching the pinnacle of their career at Arnis. They were pushed to the limits and faced with extreme conditions to test their endurance and strength. There was a reason the best Kali athletes of the world trained at the School of Arnis; it produced the best in the world.

Raines planned to give this art his all until his visa ran out or he decided to extend his stay. So, was the question did Raines have any experience in Arnis? Raines answered in the affirmative but indicated that it was not nearly the level he had witnessed. So basically, a beginner. Kind of like being on the computer.

The next day Raines went for his daily run and then ate and went to the school. The instructor gave him a pair of sticks and said, hit me, or thought it sounded like that. So, Raines swung mightily and paid for his wind up with a whack on the knuckles. The instructor also had one stick stop about one inch from his head.

Each day went by in a blur, running and practicing single stick, double stick, takeaways, and many bladed techniques. But, slowly, like each of the other arts he engulfed himself in, he'd learn it, well, at least a bit more proficiently. The instructor's acknowledgment gave him the confidence he was doing at least ok. The weeks and a few months later went by; he decided to stay for a while longer, more abuse he smiled inwardly. He paid the extra fee for up to twelve months which he thought would suffice.

Being a big man, Raines loved the movement the Arnis training gave him. He wasn't shy about mixing it up and getting hit, but the hits on his bruised knuckles became fewer in number. His disarms became something that his athleticism gravitated towards more than some of the heaven and earth stick drills. Raines stayed just another couple of months but knew it was time to move on. A small farewell in his honor made him feel like he accomplished something, or maybe it was because he graciously let them kick his butt.

Raines made a plan before the New Year and called his old friend and former sensei Tosh Yokahama in Japan about staying for a long duration to include training. Tosh was very excited to see Raines. Mr. Yokahama was an expert in all forms of self-defense and just a wisp of a man at that, kind of like O'Sensei Morihei Ueshiba, founder of Aikido. They both seemed like they were floating in their respective arts. Upon picking Raines up at the airport, they journeyed to his small home and camp; well, it seemed that way, but it was his dojo—Tosh's dwelling located close to the base of Mount Fuji just outside of Fujiyoshida City. The mountain is an ominous sight. Tosh got to work and obtained the proper paperwork for Raines to stay for five years if he wanted to. Tosh was acting as his adopted father, thereby being family. Raines knew someone owed Tosh a big favor and thus gave him what he wanted; Raines received his passport with the necessary stamps and paperwork filed accordingly for five years, giving him the sense of starting a new life. Raines, however, did find that answer to the favor referenced by Tosh. Seemingly, he had saved a high-ranking official's life several years ago from an angry mob. The life Tosh protected wanted to return the favor; if he required anything, Tosh should never hesitate to ask. Tosh told Raines that this was the moment and that this was that favor. He told Raines to forget about everything he had learned, well, maybe not the computer stuff, and Tosh laughed aloud.

The training was going quite well, moving around, getting used to new movements, and gliding, kind of like a Martial ballet. So, Raines, being lulled into an easy training session was a mistake. Everything looked graceful until the contact began.

Waking each morning in pain wasn't his idea of a good time. But his edge seemed to be back in layers. The focus of being that apex protector was becoming a reality after this long time of absence, picking himself up off from the sweat, blood-stained mat, mostly his own. Being punched, kicked, hit with weapons, and thrown around by a man half his size and moving like the wind was a daily occurrence. But the pain was overshadowed by focus and resolve to be the best he could be. His daily program also included running up Mt. Fuji.

There is a trail all hikers use, which is about twenty-four hundred meters or more from the base to the top. He started his running program up the steep path and quickly found it was much more challenging than he thought. Raines had made it to about a quarter of the way up before descending quite exhausted. After some time, he developed a fan base of onlookers on how far and fast he could make it to the top. Raines was twice the size of many who tried and failed but eventually made it. The rules are you have to do it within four hours and thirty minutes. The race has a three-thousand-meter elevation gain on the trail, a twenty-one-degree temperature drop, and the oxygen drops to seventy percent.

Raines made it halfway on his second unofficial attempt, then three quarters, and finally, the actual race was on. Raines ran steadily up the mountain. His breathing was good; some runners passed him, some quit, and some fell behind. His steady, disciplined breathing worked for him, and the oxygen was getting notably thinner. Those that fell behind cheered for Raines; their encouragement pushed him. Finally, three hours and twenty minutes later, he made it to the top, muscles cramping a little and some spasms in the legs; otherwise, he was in pretty good shape. It was the most challenging endurance training that he had ever endured. He was glad it was over only to get back down to the bottom to see Sensei Tosh commenting that it didn't seem all that tough.

Tosh smiled, and now it was time for his actual training in the dojo. He questioned Raines as to why he kept running up the hill.

Raines knew it was senseless to answer as he knew Tosh would not understand the challenge. After refueling his body with necessary electrolytes and fluids, Raines returned to the dojo. He found himself more upright lately than in the horizontal position during the combative training. Either he was getting better, or Tosh was tired of picking him up.

This training, along with academics, once again became a passion for life. The latter is what many do not know. The layperson thinks it's all about being a tough guy. Well, kids, that's the easy way out, Raines thought silently. Blood, sweat and tears, intelligence gathering, advances, and many sacrifices, are protective protocols. While daydreaming, Raines did not see the knockout blow coming from the small tornado named Tosh. Instead, Raines surmised Tosh struck on a pressure point located at the back of the neck on either side called gallbladder twenty. At least he hoped it was him. Upon waking, no one was present; the only thing stirring was the insect variety and Raines. There was no sense moving to the house; Raines slept where he was, the training floor.

As the months and years went by, the training became synonymous with living in Japan and the martial way. Tosh had trained him so and wanted Raines to live out his life here instead of searching for unattainable answers and living in a dark place again. But he felt that his student needed to do it all before he felt whole again.

So in between all the training sessions, Raines tried to reach out to see who was still working in the industry of close protection. Ed W. had passed, as did Johnny K. Others were not in the industry anymore. So, a new crop of protectors had emerged, it seems.

The year 2011 quickly became 2016. Raines's body looked like a cross between a lean bodybuilder and an Olympic decathlete. He weighed about two hundred and ten pounds now, his long hair pulled up in a top knot, and his graying beard cut somewhat close to his face with no natural fashion. However, he spoke fluent Japanese now and was proud to do some physical Olympic-level athletic skills. His computer skills still needed some work, but he kept track of global events, took many online courses, and had a mobile phone delivered to him near Fuji's base. In addition, Raines had a strong cell tower erected close by; he wanted every electronic device to work just like he did in Australia, where he had a cell tower erected to stay in touch with the world.

Raines called Mike Evans, who was, to put it mildly, shocked to hear his voice. Raines had asked how the accommodations were with his townhouse, and Mike had replied that people were renting it. The money went back into an account that Raines left opened some years ago. In addition, he had heard a rumor that he, Raines, was dead and asked where he was currently. Raines was evasive in his answer, not giving away too much too soon. He told Mike not to say anything about him being alive or returning to the States.

As Mike was giving Raines some small talk, the sound of gunfire, motors, and possible grenades were heard and echoed in the background. The explosions reverberated like thunder and shook the buildings nearby as though there was an earthquake. Raines asked Mike what was going on and where was he? Since working as a private contractor, Mike's task, or so he relayed, was to track various terrorist training camps of interest. This camp was one of them. The base was outside of Damascus, but it could have easily been any camp with fanatical beliefs against the great Satan, The United States of America. Mike asked Raines if he were coming home anytime soon. Raines had replied that it was possible and had a few things on the burner. However, Raines felt a wave of uneasiness and paranoia come over him for some strange reason. Maybe he thought it was just that he had been away for so long that he had to rebuild his trust in people and had to reconnect all over again.

Raines turned on his computer in quiet time away from training, typed in violent incidences in America, and found a few that got his attention.

An attacker killed forty-nine people with fifty-three injured in a terrorist attack at a nightclub in Orlando, Florida. The attacker was an American-born citizen with allegiance to ISIL.

The news indicated stabbings in both Virginia and Minnesota with ISIL connections.

It seems like things are getting worse, Raines thought.

CHAPTER 7

RED CARPET

Cameron fought back the crowd but felt the knife across his chest. Luckily, he had been wearing a slash-proof turtle skin undershirt, and this particular attack ruined his suit but nothing more. He had next felt the stinging of pain on his arm, and when one attacker went down, another took his place, and this time a gun appeared. Cam felt someone push him out of the way when the gun discharged. The attacker's finger was ready to squeeze the trigger once again when Cam disarmed him with the barrel pointing straight up. He jerked the gun free, most likely breaking the assailant's finger, which was still in the guard. By this time, law enforcement was on the scene and got some sense of order re-established.

Cam was standing on his assailant's ankle with the gun pointed at him. The police, not knowing what was up, took the firearm from Cameron and ordered him face down on the ground. To them, he was a culprit. However, after getting the statements and events leading up to their arrival, the police had Cameron back upright, cleared of any wrongdoing, albeit with blood dripping down his hand. Cam looked around and saw a number of his attackers in pain. Some looked as though they had broken arms, legs and some were still out cold. Others who had been knocked down were up on their feet, looking around them with a mixture of shock and confusion on their faces.

Cameron accessed the scene and discovered his agent Phil lying on the ground with an apparent bullet wound in his upper torso. Cameron yelled out to whoever was in authority; he needed an ambulance and paramedics. Phil whispered kiddingly that that's the last time he would rescue Cameron and that he owed him one. Even in pain, Phil managed to joke about it and make Cameron snicker a bit. The paramedics on the scene determined that the bullet went cleanly through Phil's shoulder, what one would call a clean exit wound. The paramedics asked Cam if he was ok because he had blood dripping on the red carpet; the irony thought Cameron was dripping red on the red carpet. He took off his jacket and had a six-inch razor cut on the inside of his arm from bicep to about midway down his forearm; his arm would need attention. He would need some stitches. They stitched Cameron on the spot and took Phil and other seriously injured persons to the hospital. Cameron called Dan, his other agent, and told him what transpired, including a bullet meeting Phil in the shoulder; things were now in a controlled mode. Dan wanted to know everything, and Cam said he would do a de-briefing shortly and sit tight. Cam also asked how R.J., the client, was doing and wanted him to participate in the briefing. After Cam gave the police his statement about what transpired, he called one of his cars to pick him up. While on his way to the hotel, turning on his phone, cracked screen and all, it seemed it had been in a war as well, he called Sara.

Sara, panicking, picked up the phone halfway into the first ring, hoping it was Cameron on the other end. It was. They both started talking simultaneously, with Sara wondering if he was ok and that she saw him on TV. Cameron told her he was ok and would be back home soon. Once the talking stopped, the silence indicated that Cameron would speak first and told her what had transpired on the red carpet.

He gave her the overview about the shooting involving Phil, and he had a nick on his arm, stretching the truth a little. Sara picked her cue that it was her turn and mentioned how she saw everything on TV and was worried; she admitted she was falling for him in a big way.

Cameron answered, "Me too," ended the call with Sara, and continued to the Four Seasons Hotel. He called Dan and asked what floor they were on as he was on his way. Upon arriving, people were all over the place as if they were doing damage control of some kind. Cameron just wanted to see the client and Dan, make sure everyone was alright, and move forward with his post-protection detail assessment.

The briefing included the client, Cameron's friend (the production manager), and Dan. Cameron told everyone that they were lucky today regarding the violence that ensued because of the client's remarks to the press before the event. He held his hand up as the client wanted to give his two cents worth. Cameron told him of the shooting and bullet hole in his teammate and that he was gashed on the arm while defending against others that wanted to do the client bodily harm. These are the things that Dan knew but no one else in the room.

Cameron continued with his briefing and indicated that if this client wanted to have experienced security, he would have to listen to their plan. However, if it required more people, the client would have to suck it up and pay for them, as he may not be so fortunate next time.

You could hear a pin drop. R.J., the client, said in a very soft voice, "I'm sorry. I really am."

The production manager and the client excused themselves to the other side of the room; both reached into their pockets and took out envelopes, presumably some money. Then, both seemed to be in a deep conversation and put some cash in another envelope. Finally, they returned to Cameron and Dan, handed Cam the thick envelope, and said, we'd like to use your company again, and we will listen to your concerns. There is enough money enclosed to tell you how much we appreciate your service, honesty, and saving our lives.

The production manager chimed in and said, 'You might want to buy a new suit, though." That seemed to break the ice. Everyone looked at Cameron's suit as there were a small number of slashes and bloodstains from his attackers, and he mentioned it would be an exciting story to tell.

With that, Dan and Cameron thanked them, exchanged numbers, and left. Cameron gave Dan a good share of the money for being there and helping during the chaos, saved some for Phil for saving his life, and then went out and got cleaned up and bought a new suit. Cam felt blessed that his turtle skin shirt offered slash and stab protection. He wanted to look good before seeing Phil in the hospital and returning home to Sara. Dan asked Cam if there was something he needed to know. He went on to say who he wants to be is ok with him. Cameron said, "What are you talking about?" It was then Cameron looked at his luggage, which was partially open, and saw a pair of black lace thong underwear hanging on the edge.

Cam laughed out loud and said, "Sara must have put them in there before I left."

Dan just nodded, not sure whether to believe him or not. "Good disguise," quipped Dan. They both laughed.

CHAPTER 8

NEW EVIDENCE

Raines wired up his devices and reached out to the NYPD Intelligence Bureau. He was told to stand by for a call from a detective who would explain where they were in the process of gathering information about the bomber behind the bombings in 1991. He reached out to the desk Sargent and told him who he was, well, kind of, and asked about the events concerning the bombing in May of 1991. Unfortunately, Det. Smith, the officer in charge of that case, had passed a couple of years ago. Det. Smith, the original officer in charge, told a new guy, before his passing, to keep working the case; he asked Raines if he wanted to speak with him. The officer in charge now is Det. Glover.

Raines tried to use a pseudonym, but the officer was not a dummy and said, "Is this Edmond Raines?" Raines said yes, gave him additional information as needed to confirm, and was transferred to Detective Glover. The officer said they had been making significant strides in that bombing incident and who was responsible. Raines broke out in a sweat and said, continue. Detective Glover then told Raines of the video and how they could enhance the images to ninety-five percent accuracy. So apparently, a female of an average build was seen carrying a baby carrier to the hotel's front door. It seems like the doorman was familiar with her, that she was a resident in the hotel, or batted her eyes as he let her leave this carrier to the left of the front door. The doorman took the baby carrier and put it inside, to his right, out of the way. The bomb squad and investigators later found traces of C-4 explosives as the baby carrier's construction and its explosive material was part of the frame. Thus, the baby carrier structure was the bomb. Next, we looked at the person delivering the package or, in this case, the baby bomb. The photo showed a female of middle-eastern descent. The image was sharpened just this week, so good timing. We have identified the suspect and came up with the following name Lash Galik, placed in the same area involving many low-level bombings in the Middle East, with no charges pending against her. We have done our due diligence and determined that this person of interest is very deadly with or without weapons. So, we are dealing with a very violent person with credentials to back it up.

"And Raines," said the detective, "She is still out there; we are having a hard time locating her travels and training. She seems more deadly now than she was in nineteen ninety-one. We will keep you in the loop, promise."

Detective Glover emailed Raines the picture and background info on this deadly individual. Raines looked at her eyes with a head covering as worn in most Middle Eastern countries; dark brown, almost black. And her eyes seemed lifeless, with no emotion. Yet, after all these years, the fact that she was still at large was astonishing. Raines reached out to Mike Evans. There was no answer, but Raines decided not to leave a voice mail.

Raines went back to Tosh, and Tosh knew something was different.

"So, when are you leaving," Tosh asked more as a father figure.

"I'm not," replied Raines, "Well, not just yet, we have a lot of training to do, and this is the best place to get it all together, both academically and physically."

Tosh said something that Raines was surprised to hear. "When you do leave, can I come with you? Someone needs to watch out for you," he said with a big smile.

"Sure," said Raines, "It would be an honor."

Together they decided to stay in Japan for another few years unless they received some hard evidence from Detective Glover. He chose not to go back to the states at this time. He did not want to be running around, not knowing when and where Lash Galik would be surfacing as she may not even be in the United States.

Raines's training again kicked up a notch as now he had to go full bore with Tosh. A younger, stronger, and experienced fighter like Raines was a tough opponent for anyone, but he needed to stay at the top of his game. Raines was unsure what dangers his future held. So, Tosh enlisted some Martial Artists from area dojo's who had no idea what level of training Raines had been doing. And vise-versa Raines was unaware of the same.

One by one, sometimes two on one, Raines being the one, they attacked with a frenzy, not wanting this Gajin, meaning outsider, to best any one of them. The invited students were smart enough to realize this was just not someone who was making his bones in Martial Arts; it was someone who broke more bones than not. Someone that Grand Master Tosh was training was not someone to take lightly. The twelve students tested Raines's endurance to test him in every way. Punching, kicking, takedowns, weapons, pressure points were part of today's intense training which would last ten hours. It's not that Raines did not get hit, but he minimized the force by turning, moving at the last moment, deflecting, and minimizing damage while administering his own. His reflexes were on point, and his defenses helped him mitigate the intensity of every attack that came his way. Some of this unarmed combat had Raines blindfolded to use his other senses. In the scientific world, it's called echolocation drills.

Weapons came out bo-staff, various blades, weapons of different lengths, such as Manriki-Gusari, a double-weighted chain; Raines handled all to the pride of his sensei. Later he would find some significant bruises, minor cuts, and achy muscles during his soak in a hot tub and cold plunge; all good; no one was the wiser. Well, maybe Tosh, as he observed Raines winced a couple of times during the fighting exercises and getting in and out of the tubs.

CHAPTER 9

BACK HOME / ON THE ROAD AGAIN

Cameron decided to surprise Sara and arrive a day early. In the driveway, he went in, all excited to feel her warmth. He could not wait to hold her in his arms and make sweet love to her. Hmm, no one home, Cam thought. That was strange. Then, he saw a flyer on the table about an M.M.A. school nearby. Sara in an MMA school? "This I gotta see," he whispered.

Cameron grabbed his gear and headed over; the worse thing was that she would not be there, and he would have gotten in a much-needed workout.

Cameron arrived at the M.M.A. school and spotted Sara's car right off. Oh, this would be fun to watch; he pulled his ball cap down over his eyes and entered the facility. The manager knew Cameron and said welcome back. Cam put his finger to his lips and said, "Shhh."

There she was, all five foot nine of her in the ring; her opponents came at her one at a time and then two on one. She sprung, kicked, swept, and flipped the most determined athletes. Mostly male. She was so extraordinarily graceful and fluid in her movements, and her athleticism was an understatement; to be sure, she kept moving. A sizeable male athlete was sneaking up on her from the back while another was distracting from the front. Sara gracefully jumped and flipped over the man facing her. The attacker to her rear caught her heel in the jaw as she was upside down. She then flipped the first attacker, much to his surprise. Cameron was more than impressed. He snuck around to the backside of the ring and entered, back facing Sara. She wasn't even breathing hard, and the two former attackers said good luck. Cameron removed his sweat jacket and turned around; "I thought you'd be faster," Cam said. Sara's eyes turned green again.

They embraced, and Sara said, "Aimeriez-vous avoir une bonne séance d'entraînement?" Her eyes were ablaze.

Loosely translated, she asked if he wanted a good workout, primarily with her.

Cam smiled didn't say a word as he led her out of the training facility and to his car. Sara left her car where it was.

"So, Sara, when were you going to tell me about your skill level? Very impressive."

Sara was about to reply when the phone rang. "Damn phone," she whispered.

"Paris, yes, sir," said Cameron. "I will be ready; please send all pertinent info that I can study in my office and on the plane."

Sara's face dropped a little, and she said, "Paris, you are just getting home and leaving again. We need time together."

With that, Cam held up his hand, a huge smile, and said, "We are going together in five days. I will be working for a few days, and since you are from there, you will know your way around. Fair enough?" asked Cameron.

Sara hugged Cameron hard, causing him to swerve and almost go off the road. "So, when do we leave? I'll need to buy some very nice outfits."

After straightening out, the car, Cam asked her what she was going to say before the call came in.

Sara looked at him in a blank stare and said, "I'm not sure pull-over. I'm going to drive," said Sara in a sexy voice. With that, they switched drivers, and Sara drove almost home; she veered left and went down a secluded dirt road towards what Cam surmised as a secret hide-away of some kind.

They both got out of the car, and Cam held out her black thong underwear and said, "Would you need these?" They both laughed.

Cam watched her disrobe totally and jump into a local swimming hole. "You are crazy," Cam said.

"Come in. The water is great," Sara said.

As she started her walk out of the water, the sun cast a light enveloping her, and its divine glow on her naked body shone a heavenly aura of some kind in an angelic way. Her hair was long, flowing, and tangled around her shoulders like a golden waterfall, reaching down to her waist.

The only words that came out of Cam's mouth were, "Wow, what a body." He saw that she had filled out a little more in all the right places, and he couldn't get into the water fast enough, where they made passionate love very much like when they first met. He would have been willing to spend every day of his life with her if only he could, but there were so many other things going on in his life right now he didn't know how it was possible for him.

After getting their clothes, well, most of them, together and checking that no one was watching, they got back in the car giggling like two high school kids who got away with something. Cameron brought Sara back to her car at the M.M.A. facility, and then both headed home.

After getting situated back in their house for a moment, Cam was the first to break the ice and went back to business mode. He told Sara that a V.I.P. from Miami, a Mr. J for short, wanted to travel to Paris for a global business meeting. They would be leaving to advance Paris with a good friend, who Cam hoped would be available; he named him Y for now.

"We will be leaving in five days," said Cameron. "Buy whatever you think you'll need for about two weeks' worth of vacation time, in the event we stay longer."

The job would also last about five days, and it would give Cameron time to advance and both of them some time to spend together before the actual assignment. After that, Sara would take up residence at the Le Warwick Hotel, and Cameron would be not that far away when he was on the clock.

From what he saw earlier, Sara could handle herself quite well, and having grown up there, she would be able to move about without too much worry. Plus, she knew the local language. Little did she know Cameron spoke fluent French as well. So, Cameron would fly with the client back to the States at least that was the current plan, tuck him safely at his home in Miami, and then make a return trip to get Sara. It seemed like a win-win, and everyone would be happy and safe.

The travel day was upon them, flying first class; they were heading to Paris. Sara was very giddy. She was going home, she thought inwardly. Cameron had called a friend named Yates to make sure all was copacetic on his end, and it was, well, almost as he was on a protective detail currently. The flight was uneventful. Cameron slept most of the way, and Sara got caught up with fashion magazines. It took about seven and a half hours, and they landed in Paris-De Gaulle Airport outside of the city proper.

The police met them upon landing; odd thought Cameron.

"Eh bien salut Sara, c'est tellement agréable de te revoir. Ça fait combien de temps, dix ans? Vous ne courrez pas sur les toits en essayant de sauver la ville des méchants, n'est-ce pas? Et qui est ton ami ici"?

(Well, hi Sara, so lovely seeing you again. How long has it been, ten years? You won't be running around rooftops trying to save the city from the bad guys, will you? And who is your friend here?)

Sara spoke English and said, "Well, good afternoon Chief Henri Phillipe-Brun, indeed it had been a long time." She completely bypassed the other part of the question. "And my friend is Cameron Stone. I am just a tourist this week. He doesn't speak French, so we'll have to speak English," she winked. Cameron smiled.

Cameron spoke up and told the chief that he was on the assignment with a client, Mr. J; he would be joining eighteen other influential leaders at a gathering at the World Conference. The chief knew of the meeting for the last couple of weeks. His concern had enough staff and resources to cover the event, not knowing what kind of security each principal had and how professional they were, so it had been a hectic couple of weeks. Cameron allowed the chief to go through his luggage, which was customary on an assignment like this for the sake of weapons, which would be a no-no under normal conditions. However, Cameron was now free to go. The chief indicated that if he needed anything (repeated it twice), do not hesitate to ask. Great to know, thought Cameron. Cameron knew that he would be asking the chief to help in many ways.

The chief offered to give them a ride to their respective hotels. Cameron agreed, knowing full well the police chief was getting his intel on where Sara was staying. She was at The Le Warwick Hotel some distance from Cam and the detail. Cameron was as transparent as he could be in outlining some details. The chief was more than happy. He did not want any global catastrophic event, anything like a terrorism-type war happening in his city. His department was also stretched by partially covering other dignitaries that would be present. So, Cam's team was welcome.

The chief and Sara headed off; it seemed like they had some catching up to do. All good. The chief indicated he would see Cam back at the hotel in about an hour.

CHAPTER 10

ALMATY, KAZAKHSTAN

The former capital of the Kazakh Soviet Socialist Republic

MODERN HI-RISE CORPORATE OFFICE

A three-vehicle SUV motorcade glided to a halt. Six booted and suited western close protection officers professionally de-bussed and escorted a male Russian business oligarch VIP towards the office. They formed a slick semi-loose formation around their client. The three drivers remained in the motorcade vehicles, engines running.

The office entrance was 75 meters away. The Anti-ram barriers were strategically placed, preventing the vehicles from gaining closer access to the office building.

There were welcoming banners and signs interspersed with Russian and Kazah national flags. Many visiting dignitaries and civilian office workers crowded around the entrance, waiting to welcome the Oligarch.

Two police vehicles parked sideways, T-bone fashion in front and to the rear of the VIP motorcade.

Many government-uniformed police officers handled the barriers, while others waited at the office entrance. They were unusually high-profile officers. Besides wearing standard-issue Soviet Makarov handguns on their police utility belts, they all carried AKSU Kalashnikovs *(cut down Kalashnikovs)* slung across their backs.

As a British close protection team commander, Yates carried a compact briefcase as he stood close behind and slightly to the Oligarch's left side. Yates's position covered half of the Oligarch's back. The front protective service officers covered the front of the VIP.

The protection detail moved in a protective wedge as the crowd began cheering and shouting their welcome greetings.

Ten meters into the pedestrian escort Yates looked uneasy. Then, with authority, he spoke into his combined radio/cell phone, "Heads Up!"

The team formation immediately closed up tighter to the VIP, as the security drivers acknowledged Marks' communication by revving their engines. Then, a smiling blond female police officer led four other police officers toward the protective service detail. She held her hand out in a welcoming fashion.

Yates was professionally paranoid; his eyes continuously scanned a 360-degree arc of observation. His cell phone ringtone quietly played the UK's National Anthem – "God save our gracious Queen, long live our noble Queen." The melody for a specific caller, namely Cameron Stone.

Yates (spoke into his cell earpiece) "Hi Cameron. Wait for five, thanks."

The protective detail was fifteen meters from the barriers and 60 meters from motorcade vehicles.

There was a distinctive sound of a Soviet Dragunov sniper rifle's 7.62 round.

Yates shouted out. "CONTACT FRONT AND LEFT!" I repeat, "CONTACT FRONT AND LEFT! GO LOUD AND TAKE COVER!"

A glance to the rear showed the middle motorcade SUV crashing into the front SUV as the driver slumped dead across his steering wheel, his foot heavy on the accelerator.

Yates raced to the barriers' cover, dropped his VIP to the ground, and covered his body. Three of his team immediately surrounded him and the VIP with their weapons drawn. The front protection officer fired his handgun into the third-floor window of the office.

The rear protection officer ran back towards the motorcade vehicle, dragged the dead driver into the front passenger well, and dove into the driver's seat. He blasted the horn three times and reversed it away from the lead vehicle.

The female police officer and her team reached across and skillfully dragged their AKSU's into a firing position. The sleeve of the female police officer rose, and Yates saw a distinctive Russian Mafia tattoo on her wrist and forearm.

The sniper fired another round into the front vehicle killing the driver instantly before the lead protection officer shot and killed the sniper. The Dragunov sniper rifle dropped and clattered to the ground. He radioed, "SNIPER DOWN, I REPEAT SNIPER DOWN. NEW TARGET ACQUISITION BOSS?"

From a kneeling position, Yates turned his briefcase to its side. He fired the concealed compact Heckler and Koch MP5K 9mm fully automatic submachine gun straight at the female police officer without opening it. Someone fell onto his body. His short burst of fire, generally a surgically accurate shot, went array. She dropped instantly, slightly wounded, fired back, and then escaped just as one of her officers tripped and discharged his AKSU wildly into an already panicking audience scrambling like rats deserting a sinking ship to get inside for cover.

Yates barked into his radio, "TACTICAL BUG OUT, POLICE ARE HOSTILES; I REPEAT POLICE ARE HOSTILES. - DETAIL MEMBERS SIX AND FIVE POP SMOKE GRENADES AND ENGAGE ANYONE IN A POLICE UNIFORM."

The distinctive short, sharp, loud report of multiple AKSU 5.45×39mm cartridges erupted as three police officers opened fire and two smoke grenades landed on their side of the barriers.

A firefight of epic proportions erupted before the protective service detail gained the upper hand by shooting all police officers in front of them.

Yates and his team conducted a rapid tactical bug out of the VIP. The unit closed ranks around him as he dragged the VIP back to the rear vehicle of the motorcade. As he threw the VIP into the car's rear, the police officer in the front police car T-boned the motorcade and pulled the pin on a Soviet grenade. Mark shouted – "CONTACT FRONT! Mark then fired five rounds from his CZ-75 handgun into the police officer, who dropped dead to the ground with the grenade locked in a death grip in his hand.

Yates shouted - "GRENADE, TAKE COVER!"

Yates dove on top of the VIP who was lying prone across the back seat of the rear motorcade vehicle as his team members instinctively sought cover positions while scanning for further threats.

The grenade detonated, blasting the police officer and the front motorcade vehicle across the tarmac.

The police officer in the rear police vehicle T-boned the rear of the motorcade, unslinging his AKSU. Two members of the protective service detail riddled him with 9mm rounds. He died before he crumpled to the ground.

Two other CPOs lifted their two dead colleagues into one of the remaining motorcade vehicles and secured the area before the vehicle housing Yates and the VIP swerved away from the kill zone.

The protective service detail conducted a tactical en-buss as their vehicle peeled away from the carnage, tires screeching hot on the tail of Yates's vehicle. Yates's phone rang. Whoever it was could have picked a better time.

Cameron into Yates's cell phone - *"You, okay? Sounds like quite a party?"*

Yates – *"Fine, Cam,"* a little out of breath; *"Just another day at the office. If we need to talk, I'll call you back."* Cameron confirmed on his end.

Yates called back about an hour later once all parties were secure and in a better place. "What's up, Cam?"

"Hey Yates, I have a project in Paris that is a real big deal. I want your help on this one."

"Sure, Cam, you wouldn't ask if it were not severe enough to have us both involved. I will be there within forty-eight hours; I have to button this one up."

So, Yates thoroughly explained that he was coming off a security detail covering four Russian Republics, Kazakhstan, Ukraine, Estonia, and Latvia. He was traveling and protecting prominent businesspersons from country to country, unsuccessfully avoiding but otherwise staying away from the bad guys, primarily the Matypes, except today. He also mentioned that although wounded, a female terrorist five foot nothing and dressed in a police uniform made her escape after the firefight.

Note to self; Trained and physically dangerous thought Cam.

Yates had answered the question about permits and clearance to carry firearms in the Russian Republic and European countries, but he knew that there would be some pushback from time to time in both areas and was ok with it. Yates would be bringing his favorite primary handgun, a Czech CZ 75 and a CZ 85 combat 9mm with an ambidextrous safety catch as his backup. Each weapon had six-fifteen round magazines brought into Paris; the procurement of weapon licensing in another country had not been an issue either.

Yates's meticulous attention to detail about his tools never ceased to amaze Cameron. While most other CPOs on the international circuit preferred state-of-the-art western handguns like Glocks, HKs, and Sigs, Yates preferred former communist block weapons when working across borders east and west European operations. His logic was simple, comm block weapons were much more reliable, and ammunition was more readily available for his operational tools. Moreover, the guns are as reliable as Kalashnikovs; drop them in the mud, water, or sand, and they still worked, unlike some temperamental modern handguns. He was keen to explain the importance considering that all ammunition was produced for sale by the lowest bidder.

Chief Brun made it back to the hotel just as Cameron started his briefing. Cameron made all the arrangements for Yates's arrival and indicated to the chief and the other CPOs that a fellow specialist would come in later and have all his permits in order. The Chief knew that Cameron was referring to firearms permits and the like. Cameron told the Chief who it was, and the Chief, amazingly enough, knew Yates. With the Chief's help getting everyone checked-in at the Citotel Aéro-Hotel nearby, including closing off floors, securing the airport, briefing the custom agents, and fortifying the hanger requirements, all had been smooth. Like Cameron, Yates was considered a very serious participant in really high-risk Close Protective services, more than Cameron on this upcoming occasion. Yates was very knowledgeable and had operational depth working dignitary protection in Paris in many instances.

Ironically, with the two of them, Yates and Cameron, it was like the cover of a well-known book Cameron thought, a gun and a katana; I think it was called The Fifth Profession.

Yates also brought a Bullet-safe 111A+ bulletproof vest. Well, he had two in his bag. Cam asked him what the second one was for, and Yates jokingly replied, well, if the first one didn't work. Then he told Cam that one was for the client. Cam then took out one of his turtle skin shirts as bulletproof vests are generally not stab-resistant and gave it to Yates. Yates then asked what happened to Cam's arm, and Cam replied it was just a scratch. Quite the scratch, thought Yates. Perhaps we will talk about it at another time.

Cam gave Yates a pre-operational briefing. The client, a very influential business person on the world stage, planned to meet with other world leaders about various financial and security-related issues. Without the client attending, the meeting would not happen. Moreover, if something were to happen to the client, it would take the world years to figure out what was needed to keep everyone on track to prevent a financial meltdown without the client's expertise on the subject matter. At least, that's what both Cam and Yates thought at the time. Although most of the world leaders had an idea of some of the agenda items, the presentation would iron out the short and long-term goals that only the client in this case knew.

The client did not want a significant show of force, but Cam and Yates knew what they had to do unbeknownst to the client and hired more professionals, "Boots on the ground" for extra eyes and ears. Get the client off the plane, check into the hotel, move to the conference center, make the meeting, and return to the FBO without incident or issue; best-laid plans.

In protection terminology, the client or principal would be flying in a G-5 corporate jet, tail number BEL 8854, into ASTONSKY Paris Le Bourget Airport, which opened a couple of years ago as Europe's leading business airport, located just a short distance from Paris. This Fixed Based Operator (FBO) focused on the customer experience; this airport offered premium services for the most demanding business passengers and crews. "Just the place we wanted," thought Cameron.

We would need every bit of this service and discretion for this project, Cam thought to himself. Yates and Cameron picked up two Texas Armor supplied-plated Suburban equipped with bulletproof glass and run-flat tires. The gas tank had an extra layer of armor and a bomb plate secured under its chassis. Also procured was another armored vehicle with the same specs; it looked like a mini-van from the early 2000s: a needed low-profile vehicle, an unassuming battering ram tank-like car if required. Only Yates and Cam knew of its existence.

The Les Salon Hoche Hotel was the hotel of choice. And Cameron, Yates, and the client worked the meeting room details on an encrypted Zoom before he departed from Miami.

Still, Yates, Cam, a few others on the team, and members of the hotel security staff, all well vetted by the Chief of Police, would be in force from the time the client arrived until departure from the airport, not just from the venue. Lessons learned from a FUBAR high-profile operation in Paris resulted in a royal family member's death. So, Cam and Yates instinctively gave themselves four days to put everything in place, make appropriate advances, run the routes, and alternate routes ad nauseam. Hospitals, obscure passages, and a safe room in a different hotel were detailed, staffed, and noted close to the airport. This safe room would be in addition to the same at the convention site.

The big day arrived, and all team members, including police, whom Cam had asked for assistance, were in place at all locations. The sky was clear, with no concerning weather looming. Cars were staged and ready with professional security-trained drivers behind the wheels. This experience also extended to the van and a nearby sedan. The sedan was made for speed also with run-flat tires.

The client landed without fanfare and reporters. Instead, Cameron and Yates exchanged numbers and names with the crew. They both agreed that arrivals, departures, and communication were paramount. Finally, all persons involved took their places; they drove the client to the hotel to settle in and rest before going to the city.

All parties arrived at the Citotel Aéro-Hotel close by the airport; all security was ready without looking like an overwhelming army of law enforcement. No check in was necessary; Cam and Yates led him to his room to freshen up and be prepared to leave in 2 hours.

Cameron and Yates checked and confirmed all locations from the hotel to the convention center. This due diligence included all sites where security had to be posted from arrival to lift off either a few hours after the convention or first thing in the morning; all areas needed to be secure to include posting security at the jet.

All seemed to be secure, and the motorcade and all participants, including the client, police with Chief Brun, and security, headed to the heart of Paris.

All checkpoints were secure. Additionally, the possible choke-points and streets of interest posted security; were confirmed as safe. All other participants and world leaders were in place at the convention site awaiting Mr. J and company.

Cam called one of his agents at the convention center for a sitrep and gave him an E.T.A. of ten minutes. The agent replied that they were ready for arrival and security was in place.

The arrival went very well; all vehicles in position for departure either on a projected departure time or for an emergency: Yates and Cam's van parked in the rear of the convention center for the same.

Yates, Cam, and others escorted the client to the convention room. Cam and Yates advanced the room. This exercise was primarily out of habit before letting anyone enter, even though Cam's security team had previously completed it.

The client was allowed in the room, and then the rest of the dignitaries followed suit. It was then Cam noticed a very concerned look on the face of the chief of police. A glance at Yates identified two issues of significant concern. First, a look of "A game-changing concern" on his face as he began scanning everyone and everything in the immediate vicinity. Second, he removed his discreet gold lapel badge and swapped it with a comparable red badge to signal imminent threat. This move would only be noticed by a fellow Special Forces CP professional. Cameron immediately recognized the operation threat level had escalated to the highest level.

A housekeeping staff member back at the Citotel Aéro-Hotel found a man shot to death. She discovered his body inside a custodial closet—two shots to the head.

The chief asked the obvious, "Did he look like a police officer?" You know, clean-cut, pretty good shape. She had replied in the affirmative.

The chief went to Cameron and said we might have a severe breach. So, he had the sergeants do an in-person roll call with their respective teams.

After more than a few expletives, Yates informed Cameron that they needed to Foxtrot Oscar ASAP; British army lingo translated to something like getting the hell out as soon as possible with a couple of expletives. Next, Cameron and Yates reached out to their respective teams, gave them each the recent intel, and asked them to document anything suspicious by way of personnel, cars, or a police officer out on his own. This warning extended to and included the personnel in the armored van on the backside and the sedan very close to the center's front entrance.

Cam and Yates conferred with each other and felt there may be more than one person of interest. They mutually agreed that operational Plan B needed to be implemented immediately on a need-to-know basis.

The chief had the hotel send him a picture of the deceased via text. While this was happening, one of his sergeants indicated that they were missing Patrolman Roy. The chief looked at the image; Roy, his patrolman, was one of his best, and with two others assigned to the client's hotel, his picture was on the phone. So, the chief sent the Paris detectives to secure the crime scene for any clues, including any video evidence.

Meanwhile, Cam called his agent at the hotel and the one assigned to the airport: no answer on either one.

Operationally, Cam called the sedan driver, plus two, and asked him to grab a local L.E.O. and get out to the airport as fast as the car would go. Secure the airport.

Exercising professional courtesy, Cameron indicated to other security teams at the conference what was happening. Then, the security chiefs each grabbed their respective clients and headed out. Cam knew in his heart that Murphy's Law had visited them. Yates whispered in his ear, "Mafoisa Modus Operandi- trust no one but you and me." That confirmed his suspicion. It was their principal that the attackers wanted. Cameron and Mark escorted the principal to the hotel's safe room, best described as a massive steel vault with fresh air exchange every 15 minutes. From the outside, it looked modern and very much like the hotel décor; after a facial recognition scan and handprint verification, they tucked Mr. Jones within.

While stationed in the back of the hotel, Cam's armed security, from Paris, was alert, armed, at the ready, and vigilant. However, two individuals came towards them who looked too casual to be back there. Jasper, the passenger in the van, opened the door, challenged them, and asked if they could help them; this was a secure ally way for pedestrians. However, Jasper couldn't help think about what happened to the posted security or police at the end of the alley. Philippe, the driver, communicated with Cam and told him they had a potential threat about to go down. Jasper rechallenged them, and then the guns came out. The attackers took cover behind some building nooks. A man rushed towards Jasper and Philippe with a knife raised to distract them from their rear. Philippe was unsure about what happened next, as the knife welder was suddenly up in the air; something was around his neck. Again, only a shadow of a movement took Philippe out of his trance. The next thing they knew, something like a stone or brick hit one of the attackers from a front angle in the head while Jasper shot the other. Again, both Jasper and Philippe looked around saw some movement but no definitive bodies in action.

Jasper called Cam directly and said, "We had three bogies down here, two in front and one in back."

Cam stated the obvious, "Define had."

Jasper described how an unknown person; could be more took out the first attacker, but neither Philippe nor Jasper saw anyone. And as well, someone had the bead on Jasper, but a rock took him out, good shot from wherever it came, and Philippe shot the last one, and yes, he's dead. Again, they both saw shadows.

"Cam," Jasper added, "We have help, and we're not certainly complaining about anything on this end. But we need to find who's pulling the strings in all this. So, we'll stay put and will keep you updated. "Oh, and Cameron, in your martial arts world, you wouldn't by any chance know any Ninjas, would you?" They both laughed, but with some interesting thought to the matter, more on Cam's end than Jasper.

CHAPTER 11

RAINES AND TOSH, 2020

It was the end of springtime, the year two thousand twenty. It was time for Raines to leave, and like he promised Tosh, his sensei was coming along and leaving his home far behind, knowing full well he would not be returning. But unfortunately, the Coronavirus 19 was starting to take a foothold in Asia, so Raines decided Australia was his first destination. So, with all their paperwork in place, plus a well-placed call to the harbormaster in Victoria, they left Japan. It seemed like they were in the air forever when they finally touched down in Melbourne. Raines hadn't been back in many years and was thankful the harbormaster was still there and welcomed Raines with open arms. The houseboat looked great; it even looked like he had made some improvements. He informed Raines that he had rented his boat, made a little income and wanted to know if Raines wanted a part of it. Raines declined the offer.

Raines introduced Mick, the harbormaster, to Tosh. "Be nice; he can kick all of our butts," Raines said to Mick.

"So, mate, how long will you be with us this time? The guys at the gym have missed you," he said with a laugh.

"So, what do you think, Tosh? After a bite to eat, we go to the gym and have a little workout," Raines said with a wink.

After dinner, Mick drove them to the M.M.A. facility where Raines worked out a few years back.

"Good evening, mates. What can I do for you?" The manager said. Then he recognized Raines, who looked about forty to fifty pounds lighter and very much in shape.

"Good afternoon, sir. Where can someone like me get a good workout? Oh, and this is Tosh, my instructor or sensei if you will," Raines went on.

The manager laughed and yelled out to whoever was listening, "The American is back."

A few newbies looked up briefly and said nothing, while the two he had an altercation with years ago mouthed the words, "Oh crap." They approached Raines with an air of trepidation, not knowing what may happen. Their faces grew tensed as they neared the very lean in shape individual and then recognized who he was. Beads of perspiration formed on their forehead as they muttered small hellos.

"Good evening, gents; we are so happy that you are still here; how are your workouts going?" Raines asked.

The one who gave Raines a broken nose spoke first and said he did not think he would ever see Raines again after the last beating he gave him. There was a sense of cockiness in his voice.

Raines shrugged it off and replied that it wasn't him who wanted to fight today; it was his teacher, this tiny, frail-looking wisp of a man. Tosh nodded and jumped into the ring. He leaped over the top rope and landed softly as a feather on the ring apron.

Tosh's hands tucked in his robe indicated to the big man, "Come, come, I don't have all day."

With that, the big man got in the ring, danced around a little as Mohammad Ali would, and said, "Come old-man, let's see what you got."

Before he even got the last word out of his mouth, Tosh was on him, hit a pressure point on his arm and head, and the would-be fighter with all the answers was out cold before hitting the mat. It was evident that Tosh was dominating the fight. He turned to the big man who now lay flat in the ring, with a grin as if he meant, "I told you so!" It had been a while since Tosh was in the field and fought someone for real. But this match was too plain for his liking; he wanted more. Tosh turned to Raines, who was working out with a Cheshire cat smile, and said, "You said he was tough."

All the patrons stood with their mouths open; they had never witnessed anything quite like that. Meanwhile, Raines had been jumping rope when Tosh's brief encounter in the ring concluded. Tosh joined him by the heavy bag and watched Raines kick and punch the Muay Thai heavy bag with controlled fury. Tosh had shaken his head once and said to Raines, "You dropped your right hand once. Haven't you been practicing?"

Raines ignored him and then went onto the treadmill and ran five miles while Tosh read a local magazine and smiled.

The manager asked if they were coming back in the morning, and the answer was yes by Raines and a shrug by Tosh.

Raines, Tosh, and the harbormaster went back to the boat, whereby Raines needed to get caught up in world events, more than the Covid was spreading. Raines tried to call Mike Evans, and again he got his voice mail; Raines did not leave a message. His instincts told him something was wrong somewhere, but he couldn't pinpoint it.

The harbormaster asked Raines if he was still doing that "body-guard thing." If so, would he want to team up with a local security group escorting a prominent business person around the city? He went on to say they could use someone of Raines's abilities. If Raines said yes, Mick would give him a number to call.

Raines was excited to get back in the fold, and after making the call, they set up an interview for him the next day.

The following day Raines met with the team leader, and all went well; Raines was designated to be the closest to the client for last line defense as Raines could not carry a gun which made no difference to him. He was happy to be a part of the group and didn't care if he ever got paid. It wasn't the money for him but the experience and the adrenaline rush he got from being out into the field and doing what he did best.

Two days later, the client came in by yacht and anchored a few spots down from Raines's houseboat, how convenient thought Raines. The motorcade came in; the client was in the middle car with Raines in the front seat. They toured around the city and parked in front of a large building structure, well massive by Melbourne standards. Drivers remained in the vehicles; Raines got out and held his hand up to scan the surrounding area, including the other side of the street. Raines indicated all was clear and secure, and they opened the door for the client. Raines stayed outside with the drivers, who were also Close Protection Specialists. The other team members escorted the client into a nearby building. Other than a few people walking the streets, nothing at this time seemed amiss. Homeless individuals occupied both sides of the boulevard, some awake, some sleeping, or no longer on this planet. This group gave Raines a slight concern, but the drivers paid no attention. Most of the homelessness was due in part to the Corona Virus.

After about two hours, the team leader indicated that the client was coming down. Drivers assumed their positions behind the wheel of their respective vehicles.

The client came out and immediately noticed one of the homeless people about forty feet away. The rag-dressed person held his hand out and asked for money to buy food. The client always tried to project the best version of himself and told his security to back away as this would be a charitable personal conversation and connection. The homeless person stood with his back to the protectors, who had seen this several times before. This simple act of resting on their laurels while he made this peaceful act of kindness would play out. The client would give the homeless person a hundred dollars a handshake, and both parties would go their separate ways. However, Raines had already moved to the other side of the street, crossed, and saw the potential attack starting to take form. There was another seemingly drunk or drugged homeless person coming out of the alley, and he saw a metal object sliding down the number two attacker's sleeve within Raines's sight. It looked like a sawed-off sharpened tire iron; he did not see Raines and focused on what the official-looking security would do. Raines almost casually walked up in the attacker's back, grabbed the weapon arm, and nearly tore it out of the socket. The security team slightly froze in place as they did not see Raines. After administering a solid hit on the back of the attacker's head, Raines held the tire iron, rendering him unconscious, and yelled "Duck."

The client took the command, whereas the security team was unsure why he yelled duck and saw Raines throw a metal object towards homeless person attacker number one, who was withdrawing a homemade knife, a shiv if you will. The tire iron hit him full force in the shoulder attached to the arm and hand holding the knife. In six steps, Raines made it to the attacker withering in pain, swept him hard to the ground, got the client out of harm's way, and delivered him to the security team, several of who were still wondering what just happened, as things happened within seconds.

Raines yelled, "Get him out of here."

Raines picked out one of the security specialists and told him to hold back with him and call the police. While he did that, Raines gathered up both individuals and propped them up against the wall. Both seemed more than a little disorientated and wounded. Their I.D.s were removed from their jackets and handed to the police after they arrived. Raines told the other specialist not to use his name as he wanted to remain as low profile as possible. Raines told the officer he had just arrived when they did and was curious about what transpired. They told him to leave as it was police business, which he did. Although they added, "Could you make yourself available if we need answers to some questions?" Raines said, "Sure," kind of fibbed a little, c'est la vie.

Raines took a cab back to his houseboat and made a little hike down to the yacht, where it looked like the security team was having a conversation or perhaps a briefing about the incident in the city.

The team leader came over, shook Raines's hand, and said, "Thanks, Raines, you saved our client: man, you move fast." He went on to add that the client would like to speak with you. Raines thanked him and found the client on the upper deck.

"Hey, Raines," said Mr. Jones, "You saved my life today, very impressive. It wasn't only what you did, but your protective intelligence was on point, how did you know?" and gave Raines a thick envelope full of money. "You are an American," Jones said it as more of a statement than a question.

"Whenever you are in New York City or Miami, give me a call; I'll have a job for you. In fact," he went on, "Whenever you go back to the states, let me know. When or if you are in the country, you will have a permanent position on my staff."

Additionally, Jones asked Raines about his projected travel in the future and offered his private jet to Raines as somewhat of a payback for saving him. "Commercial travel is significantly restricted, but give me a shout when you are ready to leave." Jones seemed very sincere about this. He told Raines that he got on his yacht when he came to Australia and toured around the different cities, mainly on the east coast. Very relaxing.

Raines stood there not quite knowing what to say, but in the end stated that Mr. Jones did have a good team here and that he, Raines, just happened to be in the right place at the right time. He also mentioned to Mr. Jones that he took commands very well and ducked. Almost like he'd been in many situations like this before. Raines also told him he was from New York, and if Mr. Jones were serious, he would look him up when he was in the U.S.A. in about a year. With that, Mr. Jones smiled, gave him a firm handshake, gave Raines his business card, and said thanks. So, Jones was a man of few words; Raines thought, instinct, and paranoia crept into his subconscious mind. I need to do a background on him.

Raines walked off the boat and said to the team leader, "When the team is ready to take a break, meet me at the seafood place called the Ocean Crest Café one block down. My treat, we can eat in two or three shifts, up to you, mate."

The team leader talked to the client about the eating plan, returned to his team, and said, "You heard the man," he handpicked a few of the team, and they followed Raines. Later all three groups had their fill and thanked Raines.

Raines asked the team leader to borrow his phone and dialed Mike Evan's number. Someone had picked up, but all he heard was gunfire and a female voice shouting. The call ended. Raines wondered if it was Lash Galik; perhaps the thought was wishful thinking and farfetched. He dismissed another idea in his mind but noted it for now.

CHAPTER 12

SARA-
HOMECOMING

Sara's ride to the Le Warwick was full of answers to the barrage of questions from Chief Brun. First, she promised to behave herself and stay out of trouble; indeed, he nodded, but he wasn't buying that, plus Sara had her fingers crossed. So instead, she told him that she would be spending her free time with her friends in the city, getting her exercise running and her favorite, parkour.

Sara got her bearings in her new surroundings and a day later called her friends, who were thrilled to hear from her. They asked if she had been practicing, and she replied yes, but a lot more; she told them about Cameron and their relationship. She also indicated to them why she was there in the first place. Most of her friends had heard of the world conference taking place and the potential for Murphy's Law.

Sara's friend picked her up, and they went into the heart of Paris. There was an area where they used to practice, and they began leaping over things like old times. One of her colleagues just stood there admiring Sara's improved skill; she had become much more an athlete and more adept in applying her moves to all obstacles. They were impressed. It seemed as though there wasn't anything she couldn't do. One might think that Sara's skills might fade with time, but it only appeared as if she had been practicing full-time. Perhaps she had been training with someone with a higher level of skills, one of her friends thought. That seemed the only logical explanation for Sara never going out of practice,

"So, let's play in the actual city where we may see some things play out." Her parkour partner kiddingly said.

She was, as everyone guessed, back to her old self in trying to play Ninja, and they all agreed she very well might be.

They all dressed alike, more to keep Sara out of trouble, and it was more challenging to identify a singular person. Hoods came in handy.

The Parkour team heard cars driving faster than usual within city limits, sirens blaring. They posted themselves on different buildings and communicated their observations. Pretty cool view thought most of the team, whereas Sara knew something was unquestionably wrong. Cameron taught Sara well. When everything was successful, all seemed dull ninety-five percent of the time to the general public; otherwise, preparing for the other five percent of terror was crucial during training exercises. Sara and company kept a low profile as they neared The Les Salon Hoche Hotel, where the conference was going on. Too much activity, thought Sara; something was wrong. No snipers on the rooftops that she noticed. Instead, Sara observed a van positioned on the backside of the hotel. Most likely a non-descript, heavily armored escape vehicle, she knew the lingo and was quite proud of that. She knew it was someone from the good guy group.

Sara watched with curiosity as two men approached the vehicle and did not stop when challenged. She then observed another individual sneaking up on the car from the rear. Sara lowered herself down from the top of the building and took out a weighted rope that, on this day, would be a weapon, not a climbing tool.

The man sneaking towards the vehicle broke into a run and started yelling wildly, distracting the van driver and his partner. Sara threw her rope, weighted end first, at the man's head, it wrapped around the attacker's neck, and Sara, partially hidden in a nook, jerked it hard. Because Sara was about ten feet above the attacker, it seemed as though he just floated magically upwards and then dropped when the rope took hold. Sara disappeared but not before she saw a rock or some blunt object take out one of the bad guys approaching the van, and then the shot was fired, taking out the other one.

Sara couldn't wait to get out of there; her heart was beating hard, her adrenaline made her move faster, her anxiety levels peaked, she was not used to this type of thing. But, Cameron lived in this world. Is he insane, she thought? So, Sara and her parkour teammates gathered away from it in an area they called their playground to catch their breath.

Then, Sara's phone rang; it was Cameron.

Sara answered and said, "Hi honey, how are things? I thought you had an assignment today. Are things going well?"

Cameron replied, "You sound like you are out of breath; you weren't in the city today, were you?"

"No," lied Sara, "We have been here practicing, vaulting, and doing our general gymnastic type program using building structures. So, we were just finishing up. What happened?"

"Well," Cameron went on, "Whoever it was, saved a couple of lives. So, we wanted to say thanks but be cautious."

The line went dead.

CHAPTER 13

"MURPHY"

Cam heard Sara on the phone, but the call went dead. Unfortunate, he thought to himself, and there's nothing I can do about it now, which is generally why an agent would not take a loved one on an assignment like this. For Sara, though, it was home. How much trouble could she get into, he thought? The assignment was not going as planned; they needed to develop a defensive plan that may turn into an offensive one. The latter would not be a wrong choice now as it beat sitting around waiting for something to happen.

Cam called the sedan, which could be at the airport. The driver, Ian, answered immediately and indicated that there was nothing suspicious to report, but no security personnel was at the hotel, and the police had just arrived. Ian further went on to say that they were heading to the airport hangar and would report their findings. They arrived at the hangar and waited outside the door where the jet was secured. Ian called the captain, who responded rather quickly. The pilot acknowledged that everything was good. Ian asked if he could come down and let them in; there was a hesitation on the other end, and he said he would be down in a moment. Ian set up a perimeter as things didn't feel right. Instinct. The door opened but not all the way. Ian didn't hesitate to kick it in, knocking down the pilot and surprising other behind-the-door occupants. There were two of them. Ian shot the first one on the right, and an L.E.O. went on the left and shot the other. The captain, although very shaken, was the first to speak and said, "Thanks."

"Any more bad guys?" asked Ian. And added, "Are you ok?" in a concerned tone. They could not afford risking the plan any further than it had already been.

The captain replied that there were no more than the two, both shot and killed and mentioned that his co-pilot was tied up upstairs.

Ian and one other went to the upper level of the hangar. The rest of the team posted on the lower level and outside, securing the captain and the jet. All was clear on the upper level as Ian untied the co-pilot. Next, they needed to check the jet's equipment for timed explosives and tracking devices. Ian called Cam and told him that all was secure, and the plan was complete for giving the plane a thorough check for anything that did not belong or would make it falter. Ian wanted to know if there was another plane available that they could use to be on the safe side? Cam conferred with Yates, and the second idea was a strong possibility. Yates and Cam told Ian to get the second plane ASAP without giving it too much thought.

Back at the hotel, Cam and Yates got access to the safe room with the client; first, they planned to view the twenty monitors scanning the inside and out of the hotel, including the backside of the building, for other suspicious activity. Then they would literally get out of "Dodge," as they would say. All this time the client accompanied Cam and Yates and was much help in finding any loopholes the team would have left in the process.

The cameras seemed eerily quiet. Nothing was stirring. Then seemingly out of the shadows, a man, who appeared to be a police officer, uniform and everything, rounded the corner to the backside of the hotel/center and strode to where Jasper and Philippe were. Cam called Jasper and gave him a heads up that they should challenge him. Philippe got out of the car and told the officer to halt. Instead, the officer said something in French that Philippe could not understand and stepped out a little further and said halt. Then, the attacker drew his weapon faster than the eye could track, and the bogus cop shot Philippe. Jasper returned fire but missed the allusive target.

Cam felt the need to help his teammate and went out a secret staircase leading out to the back alleyway in a hidden recess in the building structure leading to the back of the van. Unfortunately, Cam didn't have a gun; shameful, but he did have a couple of throwing daggers. While the exchange of gunfire continued, Cam slipped to the other side of the street, got a bead on the target, and launched two of his throwing knives, one after another. Unfortunately, the target moved at the last second; the knives missed, and the intended target returned fire in Cam's direction. Cam ducked out of the way only to see the attacker move in a zig zap pattern and disappear into the shadows. Cam took chase, and once he got to the end of the alleyway, there was nothing there but the police uniform on the ground; no one else in sight. Cam called Yates and asked if he saw anything. Yates's first response was, you should have brought a gun, but added its impressive what you can do with those throwing knives of yours. The cameras did not pick up any movement on the streets or otherwise, and it looked as though he had disappeared into thin air.

Cam looked up and down the street for movement; no one spotted. But, again, someone couldn't disappear that quickly without being seen by the human eye or high-end cameras picking up and scanning the outside streets. There was nothing moving, human or otherwise. He wasn't sure, if anyone would believe him if he were to narrate the scene.

"Keep your eyes open, stay off the X and be careful. The attacker is a highly trained person. Something about how he moves," Yates had continued, "Military-type movements with unusual stealth-like abilities. Cam, I need you up here; all hands-on deck and required for projected exfil from the hotel."

It was then Yates spotted what appeared like a wall moving; maybe it's the cameras, he thought. Everything was still, nothing moving. This time, a person bolted across the street into a nearby alleyway that was a two-way alley as the car's movement was seen on the peripheral exiting. Automatic gunfire erupted from the vehicle aimed towards Cam's location as he hadn't quite gotten into the building yet. The car was too far away and somewhat out of the camera's range to pick up a plate number or other identifying marks. Yates saw Cam move and dodge out of the way of the hail of bullets; nine lives was the first thing that entered his mind. With the car long gone, Yates had spotted something that he wanted Cam to investigate.

"Cam check over by the corner of the building, second one down on your side," he directed. "Ok, stop right there. I see something with a slight reflection; tell me what that is."

Cam picked up what looked like a piece of stiff material, almost like a shield, "What the heck is this?"

"Ok, Cam, I want you to hide behind it and back up against the building." Just what Yates had surmised, it was an invisibility shield/fabric made for the military. It was called "Quantum Stealth." It is an invisibility cloak of sorts. Cam thought this was so cool. He had never seen anything like it. Yates spoke, "Ok, Cam, quit drooling over it and bring it up here; we'll most likely use it soon."

Cam headed back up to the safe room with his new toy, still quite amazed at the technology. As well-equipped as Cam was with guns and knives, he failed to understand the fast-moving technology. The Quantum stealth shield fascinated him and he could not wait to learn more about it. Yates had heard of the material but never seen it in person, which was impressive; he kept his drooling under control. Meanwhile, Yates had scanned the back lot to see how everyone was. Unfortunately, Philippe took a hit but would live; soon, he had to get some medical attention. Jasper stopped the bleeding, plugged the hole in his right lung, and called for an ambulance. We will need to get someone to partner up with you on the backside until we move. Yates called two of the agents to assist. Up until now, they were in the Suburban's out front and slightly out of sight until unquestionably needed. One of the agents he needed with Jasper, and the other he needed with Philippe on the way to the hospital. A personal mission is done and done.

Yates also called Ian at the airport and warned him of the possibility that a dark sedan may be coming in their direction; the passenger, if seen, was very dangerous and pissed. Ian returned with a message received and told them of the good news. They were in luck; Ian had obtained another jet, fueled and ready to go. Mr. J's plane was given a thorough once over so far with nothing to report. Cam gave Yates a thumbs up; meanwhile, the client sat there through all this violence and planning. He finally spoke up.

"Gentlemen, I have been watching the two of you go back and forth, putting yourself in harm's way to ensure I am safe. You both have contingency plans for all possible "What if" situations; have you worked together before? At first, I told you that I did not want a big show of force; thank you for not listening to me." Mr. J seemed genuinely humbled. "It seems like many good men died today in the line of duty. I want to do something for their families; I have the funds to do so." Everyone nodded as it was a very generous offer.

Cam was first to speak and said, "Thank you, but we are not out of the woods yet, sir; we need to get you back on your plane and get you home safely. So, we'll shake hands when that happens." Do you have anyone in N.Y.C. or Miami that you could use for personal security, and if not, we can offer protection?"

Yates agreed on all points and told Mr. J. he was in excellent hands with Cam. Cam had someone on the other end that could receive Mr. J. with no question about integrity.

Mr. J. added, "About a year ago, I bumped into a protector trained like yourselves who saved my life in a big way. I owe him. His name was Edmund something or other; I have his card at home. If he is not available for some reason, I will be in touch with you and listen to you both. Thank you."

CHAPTER 14

TIME TO MOVE

Raines and Tosh continued to train as though their lives depended on it physically. They got up early, had breakfast, and went straight back into the gym with a full bag of equipment which they used throughout the day in several different ways: running with a weighted vest, doing pushups on a stability ball, jumping rope; weighted, squatting, ab exercises of all kinds and pull-ups with the vest. This was followed by hundreds of kicks and punches and intense work on the Wing Chun wooden dummy and Muay Thai bag. Raines studied world events, mainly terror incidents. Seemingly time went by in a flash. The New Year and beyond came and went. Covid 19 was still with us. Most of the world had come to a standstill, but there were still terrorist activities plaguing many. The call Raines made to Evans months ago bothered him. So, he had to develop a plan, something much unexpected. He decided to call Detective Glover.

"Detective Glover? Raines here. I have an enormous favor to ask," Raines told Glover the plan and its many layers of secrecy and acting. Many people thought Raines was deceased as no one had heard from him or seen him in quite a while. So, Raines said to Glover, "Let's let them believe that."

Glover then filled him in about the woman Lash Galik. "According to our intelligence, she's been actively doing terrorist training exercises in Libya, and she has had a lot of help lately. She also may be connected recently to the attempted assassination of a high-ranking businessman in Russia, specifically in Almaty, Kazakhstan, the former capital of the Kazakh Soviet Socialist Republic. She, although wounded by the protection team, escaped. There is no worldly news at this time of her whereabouts.

There seemed to be a build-up of teams of hired killers. "So, Raines, I will keep you in the loop if I hear about this female panther of sorts. We'll get her," Glover added.

"What's a good working number for you lately?" He then went on to say there was also an attack by an unknown team in Paris, but this time, it was a male terrorist who escaped. The clients were unhurt. The protection team was well trained, led by a young protector and a veteran by the names of Cam and Yates, respectively. Raines knew of Yates but did not know a protector of an extremely high caliber named Cam, maybe short for Cameron.

Then he said, "Oh Raines, I forgot to tell you we may have some information on your son after all these years."

Raines had already hung up. Nevertheless, Raines was as ready mentally and physically as he ever was for his eventual face-off with his family's killer.

He called John Tannon about his plan. John was silent for a minute. Then, finally, he spoke softly, "And Raines, I thought...."

Raines answered his partial question and said, "That I was dead. So here is the scoop," said Raines. "We put out a press release from here in Australia that I had been shot and killed in the line of fire while on protective detail. A person who owes me a considerable favor will be sending a jet to pick up my remains. I need you to arrange for my funeral and give a big speech, make me sound like God. On the Gulfstream-5 that we will be using, another passenger will be on board, my friend Tosh, a little guy who moves like the wind. The plane is on its way right now, so expect me back at Teterboro FBO in a few days. Oh, and John, in a private trust and my last will, my townhouse goes to my son wherever he is, and if he is no longer with us, my heart is conceding that the house is yours; otherwise, you are the executor. I have a big plan in mind, and it involves taking out evil people once and for all. Are you in?"

"Sure, Raines," John answered. "How will you bypass customs?"

"All taken care of, I will give you a heads-up when we leave, tail number, and specs. I would also want you to go to the townhouse in the Village and check for listening devices, do a complete sweep, and make it your home for now; thanks. Don't stress. I will fill you in on everything, and John, I have been OK. Thanks for asking." Both enjoyed a good laugh.

CHAPTER 15

SURPRISES

So, the plan was to move the client back to the airport, secure him and make sure he landed on the other end safely. Cam and Yates had a stand-in for the client with security, who would go out the back door to the waiting armored van with Jasper. At the same time, Cam and Yates would go out the front door to the waiting Suburbans with someone dressed as the client. It wasn't Cam or Yates but two specialists similar in height, weight, and mannerisms. There would be no doubt if ever there was going to be a firefight, now would be the time. Yates and Cam waited with patience while everyone played out their parts. Everyone had rehearsed their body language several times to make sure nothing seemed out of ordinary. Minutes ticked by, but there was nothing to report on either end. So far everything was going as per the plan. Finally, Yates and Cam decided to go out the front door with less chance of being trapped and caught in a crossfire in the alley.

No sooner had they cleared the front area to the center and made their way to the vehicles with heads down than a shot rang out; the bullet ricocheted off the building twenty feet above them with no one hit, and then silence.

Cam and Yates looked up to the building tops and scanned for snipers. Because of the bright glaring sunlight directly in their eyes, they did see some rooftop movements but not enough, even wearing their Ray-Ban RB3025 Original Aviator 58mm. Sunglasses showed nothing. Note to self, Cam thought, move people early morning or evening hours to avoid any attention from the public's eye plus it's safer that way. Throw on a hoodie, a pair of glasses and you're good to go.

Then about fifty feet from their location, something fell off the rooftop of the building; it was a sniper rifle. Cam said, cover me, so Yates had him covered. Cam came back with the gun; it was a Barrett M82. Quite the military rifle, they both thought out loud. Cam glanced up to the rooftop again and saw a figure standing erect. Yates raised his gun, and Cam gently lowered his arm and said, "She's with us." The figure removed her hood and long blonde hair cascaded down over her shoulders, and as well, three of her friends stood by her side. They were all dressed in black – much like ninjas from an action movies. You could tell from their physiques even a distance away with no sun glare, that they were either well-conditioned athletes, fighters or some-one who works out for a living never mind leaping from building to building.

Cam told Yates, "That, my friend is Sara, the woman I have been telling you about." Cam waved, gave her a thumbs-up, and then pre-pared to drive to the airport.

Sara had bound the unconscious shooter with zip ties and had one of her male friends call the local precinct and tell them the location and medical condition of the person in question. The shooter was out for a while as Sara had first surprised him when he pulled the trigger; thus, the shot went array. She then kicked him in the back of the head leaving him unconscious.

There was no time to stop; they all got into the vehicle and headed to the airport. They called Jasper in the van, told him of the plan, and suggested joining them. Jasper came out of the alley and pulled up in the back of the two Suburbans. They reached out to Ian and asked him if the area was still secure and had he acquired a fast replacement jet to take the client back to the states. "All safe and confirmed," replied Ian.

The client's phone rang, and upon answering it, Mr. J's face took on a somber appearance. The client opted for the new plane and told his retained pilots to fly to Melbourne, Australia.

"Everything ok, sir?" asked Yates.

Mr. J. replied, "While protecting someone, the gentleman that saved my life a year ago took one for his client and died. The attacker's bullet passed under his arm, and the vest did not protect him. The call was from the team leader who handled my security needs in Melbourne, Australia. One of his final requests was to ship his body home to N.Y.C. It's the least I can do."

Yates spoke first and asked, "What was this gentleman's name again?"

"You probably don't know him; his name is Edmund Raines," Mr. J. stated. "Incredibly gifted."

Yates, "Wow, I have heard of him. Great guy with unquestioned integrity and no one better to have on a team. Raines, a solid individual, very well trained, disappeared some years ago when a terrorist killed his family in a '91 explosion in N.Y.C."

Mr. J continued and said, "I owe him my life. I will be sending my jet to pick up his remains and bring him back to New York." Mr. J kept shaking his head, and they thought they saw his eyes fill up.

Yates and Cameron both looked at each other. Their instincts told them there was more to this Mr. J than he might be telling them, or it's just occupational paranoia.

"Ok, you heard the man, let's get this plane ready to leave for Australia. Everything checks out, nothing suspicious?" asked Cameron. Everyone gave a thumbs up.

All technicians gave the G-5 bound to Melbourne and the other jet destined for Miami another thorough check, and all systems were technically sound. Thumbs up on all accounts. Cameron conversed and confirmed with the client that a team was in place to receive him on his arrival in Miami. The answer was in the affirmative.

Within the hour, both Jets went on their respective journeys. Cameron, Yates, and others on the team, including the Chief, shook hands and thanked each other for this challenging assignment.

Within a short time, the Chief got into his vehicle and left to reclaim his city, clean up the carnage, schedule press conferences to the world, and explain what happened and who was responsible. Moments later, Jasper waved to all as he drove away.

Yates and Cam turned to each other to go over what was next, including some professional small talk with a chat of gratitude, then a massive explosion ripped through the silence. Utterly engulfed in flames were Jasper, his partner, and the vehicle. Yates gasped in shock as the color from his face drained.

Cam's phone rang, thinking it was Sara; Cameron, not in a good place, said, "Now is not a good time," and hung up.

CHAPTER 16

TIMELINE: PRESENT DAY

The female assassin's movements needed to be careful and strategic to avoid leaving Almaty, Kazakhstan. First, she obtained various forged passports from the United States, Canada, and the U.K. Her physical characteristics and names were different on each passport, as credit cards were all legit for all her counterfeit personalities, emphasizing the latter. So, she chose the U.K. passport with blonde hair and blue eyes but nothing noteworthy that anyone could say anything but "Five-foot-five-ish blond hair blues eyes." Next, she used contacts to cover her lifeless hard blue, almost black irises. Next, she booked a flight to Gatwick Airport in London. She then booked a flight to Manchester, New Hampshire, U.S.A, rented a car, and traveled to N.Y.C. Her new name was Lynn Grey; she would then change it to another name once she disappeared with a new set of credentials, credit cards, and looks to match.

In a coordinated movement with Lash Galick's undertaking, the unknown terrorist in Paris posed as a businessman from the U.S., got on a plane at De Gaulle Airport, Paris, and headed straight to N.Y.C.

They would eventually meet up for their most significant terrorist activity ever.

Though he failed in his quest to assassinate the lead person at the convention center, he did find out a lot about the security team allocated to him and, at the same time, not being the wiser as to who he was. He had to admit that they were outstanding in the tradecraft, but pictures of most of the detail members gave him time to research their strengths and weaknesses for a future projected assault. He even dared to call one of the protectors and wanted to talk with him, but the fool hung up. Perhaps the person he wanted to speak with was expecting a call from someone on a more personal note; that feeling would need investigation.

The Gulfstream-5 aircraft from Paris to Melbourne with one stop in Singapore was on its way to pick up the remains of Raines along with a sole passenger named Tosh with a return trip to New York City. So, they should be departing Melbourne in a few days. In Melbourne, the lead security person on the team that Raines was active with closed all of Raines's affairs and put him in a safe house, away from the public eye. The local funeral director put together an altered casket that Raines would need. All documents, such as a death certificate, were in order. However, the name changed to Edward Raynes if anyone was monitoring. Once he boarded the plane, Raines could get out of the casket and tell the captain in confidence what was happening; otherwise, he would be very uncomfortable with about twenty hours or so of lying in the coffin. The long flight would not include layovers and refueling, not to mention he would have a lot of explaining to do. Everyone had their fingers crossed that the plan would work out without too many glitches. They'd put too much time and resources into making this plan successful. Mr. Jones seemingly had paved the way for much of it so that he could travel with few questions. The advantage was that Mr.

Jones thought Raines was dead. He'd have much to explain when the time came.

Back in Paris, Yates and Cameron enjoyed one last meal together and complimented each other on the missions and successes, and discussed some things that would need improvement. They knew they would require more physical training, better equipment, and a lot of mental recharge before setting off on their next mission. They lost some good men, and they did not find out who the mastermind was behind all the attacks—time to take a breath. Yates knew that he would be face-to-face with the one who got away in the firefight in Kazakhstan one day.

The only argument was who would keep the invisibility shield; what a find. Cam won on the coin flip and had the Chief get it specially packaged for customs and the flight home in a couple of days. After that, both knew they would see each other again, most likely on a protection detail and as comrades in arms.

Later in the day, Cameron called Sara and said he would join her at the Le Warwick hotel in about an hour. He also apologized for hanging up on her. She replied that it wasn't her. Cam mentioned that he had a call and thought it was her, but now he'd need to call the number back. He had his suspicions. He immediately called the number back, and the recording was in French, but the number was no longer in service, a burner phone to be sure. Anyways, he'd look into that later. He needed to spend his time off with Sara.

Cameron booked their flight home for two days from now and joined Sara.

What a reunion, Victoria's Secret and all; his first thought was that her hormones must be on overdrive. Their romantic getaway was followed by intense lovemaking with little to no breaks during the entire trip. In contrast, he was coming off a very stressed protection detail and mentioned that he needed a little more time to decompress. So, she gave him five minutes.

CHAPTER 17

DEADMAN WALKING

After a refueling stop in Hawaii and clearing customs on the plane, the dogs sniffed out possible drugs with agents checking for contraband of any kind, confirming and briefly viewing the body.

Tosh said, "Hold your breath," in Japanese. The custom agents asked what he said, and Tosh replied that it was a prayer concerning evil spirits. After that, all other official security checks were completed with no issues. The G-5 was on its way to Teterboro, NJ, USA. At the time, Raines made a call from the plane to Tannon.

"Hey John, how are things? We should be arriving about 6 pm your time this evening. Everything in place?" Raines just needed a confirmation. "Let Glover know I will call him tomorrow and touch base under the name Sam Sullivan." Tannon was still getting used to hearing Raines's voice after all these years.

"Will do, and yes, all is well and ready for your arrival. We have the hearse and a van ready for your luggage." (This was code for the body), in case anyone was listening.

The jet arrived a little early due to a good tailwind, but the hearse and van were there with John Tannon at the ready.

Raines's relationship with John was solid as he got him in the business many years ago with no hick-ups. And there were no trust issues ever. Along the years they'd become good friends and developed a bond that went beyond a regular friendship.

The conveyor belt was wheeled up to the jet's door, ready to receive the casket but not before Tosh got off and nodded to Tannon. Finally, the lift was in place, and the captain slowly got the coffin in place for a gentle descent to ground level, which was transferred to a dolly for easy transport to the hearse. Then, out of eyesight, Tosh disengaged the latch to the bottom of the coffin, and Raines slowly lowered himself to the ground and rolled under the van. The only people present were the hearse's driver, whereas, in reality, it was Detective Glover and Raines's friends John Tannon and Tosh. A small gratuity was given to the airport personnel for their assistance, taking their eyes off the van for just a moment as Raines climbed into the sliding doors on the other side of the van with blackened windows. It was the perfect plan with a perfect disguise that they pulled off without anyone knowing.

Detective Glover went to the van to get further instructions, reached his hand inside, looked in, and said, "Hi Mr. Raines, I mean Mr. Sullivan, we finally meet. I will give you what I can from the intelligence dept; for your information, we think your most wanted girlfriend was involved with an incident in Russia not long ago and could be heading to the U.S. She seems to be working with someone, but we are unsure who that individual is currently. I will hopefully see you tomorrow. Welcome back."

Raines was pleased with Glover's information and even more so that he was driving the hearse.

The small motorcade waved to the FBO workers and headed into the city. They settled on a crematorium in Elmhurst, NY, to cremate the empty coffin, no questions asked. The burial and graveside services would be at St. Micheals the next day at five pm; it's where he buried his wife some thirty years earlier.

Raines wiped all the wax-like substance off his face, making him look dead. Tosh thought it looked better on than off. After getting the urn with some other person's ashes within, they headed to Raines's place in the village.

John Tannon's first comment was that he had never seen Raines so lean and in shape. But then he looked at Tosh and asked what he had been feeding Raines and said he wanted some. Tosh shrugged and blew it off, but he was very proud of what his student had accomplished in training.

Next, Tannon spoke up and told Raines that he had found multiple listening devices in his house but uncovered nothing else. Finally, they arrived at the location. All seemed just as Raines had left it many years ago. They all looked around for anything suspicious, and Tannon gave Raines an all-clear.

Across the street, down a few houses, blue eyes spied through a set of binoculars the group entering the house. Although she and her male colleague had recently occupied it, no sound was coming through her earpieces, but then, it dawned on her that someone in the group most likely had removed the listening devices.

This fact concerned her, and she asked herself who the other men were other than who had ownership? Namely John Tannon. She took some pictures of the four individuals and had to call her partner and say to him, "I knew John lived there, but should I be concerned about the other three? Did I miss something important?" She described John Tannon as a man who looked like a cop, a taller individual with long unkempt hair, along with a much smaller individual who could be a child. Unfortunately, she couldn't tell as the latter was wearing a hooded garment. Her partner didn't know of any other persons involved.

John, Raines, Glover, and Tosh felt the same thing. Someone indeed was watching. Raines said, "Let's pretend we are going through our daily business."

John told Raines there was a car in the enclosed garage if he needed to use it. A black Shelby Cobra, 500 horsepower. Maybe one of us should take it for a spin and see what happens. Everyone nodded. John slid into the driver's seat, the garage door opened, and he flew out of there, wanting a chase. Detective Glover, Tosh, and Raines each looked around from the inside. No one moved.

Across the street and down a few houses, the blond-haired, blue-eyed woman felt a trap and did not budge. Then, about an hour later, the mustang came back, and Tannon got out of the car with a case of beer, like they were going to have a party or something. Then, a short time later, the front door opened, and a figure came out and got into the van with John just before shaking hands with the occupants inside, making it look like they hadn't seen each other for a while and would see him soon. It seemed casual enough.

Blue eyes was angry at herself for feeling on edge, more so than in the past. It was the first time in a while that there was any emotion. A small part of her even felt it was good to feel something. Too much time away from the action, her senses had dulled. Blue-eyes called her primary contact and wanted a pick-up in the middle of the night to get away for a little while. He told her he would put spotters at the house to report back, and she could be back in the city tonight to plan their event to disrupt the entire metropolitan area. He reminded her that they were getting paid fifty million dollars, a lot of money to make sure they got it right. He reminded her that he had a funeral to attend the following evening at five pm and wanted to appear under the radar with a very discrete profile. He obtained the information serendipitously from another contact he had just called for an unrelated matter.

Later, while spotters were dropped off in the middle of the night and blue eyes was picked up, all parties noted that the neighborhood was very tranquil.

"Keep your phone on and call me with any, I mean any suspicious activity," the man in the dark sunglasses went on.

Meanwhile, Tosh watched all this activity and, about an hour later, quietly slipped out of the house, crossed the street, and went to the backside of adjacent homes, one of which had a dog. Tosh had a handful of meat with a sleeping agent. The dog barked once it settled down and then was out. After that, Tosh moved to the house where the spotters were. He silently broke in and stood still for fifteen minutes with no movement. The television was on, and both occupants were more interested in the program than spotting a frail-looking man with make-up to make him look much different. Tosh subdued both, zip-tied their legs and arms, and put duct tape on their mouths. He grabbed their mobile phones, wallets, and weapons. To explain this one, he would like to be, as they say, a bird on the wall, or maybe it was a fly on the wall.

Raines woke early, expecting to see Tosh meditating, but no, Tosh was fast asleep, and Raines didn't want to wake him. So instead, Raines wondered how his funeral had gone and checked out the house and its modifications, making it a virtually impenetrable safe house.

Raines was impressed with the thick bulletproof windows, steel, Kevlar-lined walls, and a front and back door to withstand serious explosions. The basement had the same type of door leading down the stairs with a bunker feel to it, significantly reinforced, and it also included a small gym set up; he remembered all this. Raines thought, yes, the comforts of home. He remembered when he bought the house that this bomb shelter was constructed in the early sixties when there was fear that Russia would target the United States via the Cold War. The heavy steel door on the west end of the basement would go nowhere as Raines couldn't quite remember that door being down there. He opened it, and it led to a tunnel of sorts.

Perhaps going through all the depression years, I was oblivious to this tunnel, Raines thought. He shone his flashlight down through the tunnel, and it was quite a distance to the projected end. Raines would have to check and ask John about this later. Upon going back upstairs, he saw Tosh drinking a cup of tea; otherwise, he seemed very much at peace, which made Raines a bit nervous.

Raines played along, "So, Tosh, what's going on? How did you sleep?"

Tosh smiled and emptied his bag of goodies for Raines to see. Two phones, four guns, a pager, and two wallets came out.

"Where did you get all this stuff, Tosh?" Raines was surprised, impressed, and needed all the information the little guy could give.

Tosh shrugged, "I went on a scavenger hunt last night and found these items. Good job, yes?" He also mentioned that two individuals were tied up and secured.

Raines knew he wouldn't get any more info out of Tosh, so he said, "Yes, great job."

Raines reached out to Tannon and Glover and told them what he had. They both knew better than to ask how he had come in possession of such items. They told him they would be there in a couple of hours. Once Glover showed up, he could run the names and fingerprints on the guns as Tosh had put them in bags and took the would-be spies into custody.

One of the phones rang that Tosh had obtained; Raines answered it and whispered, "Can I help you?"

"Who is this?" said the voice on the other end.

Raines thought he recognized the voice on the other end but could not be sure.

"We are or will be compromised," said the sun-glassed man to his blond-haired, blue-eyed female assassin. "We can't go up and pick up our men as chances are the police are most likely doing that right now. So, we sit, wait, and see what shakes out. Our plan is still on; perhaps just lay low for a bit," he said with no hesitation or doubt.

The gravesite services scheduled for Edmond Raines at St. Michael's Cemetery were for five pm. There was a small stone with his wife's and son's names. His son Michael's had no date carved. There was a sizable crowd, and John Tannon gave the eulogy, which high-lighted Raines's life and how many people he saved along the way. He said Raines died with what he loved to do, putting others' lives before his own.

A young man stood at the cemetery and off to the side; he had dark hair and a faded scar running from his forehead and framing his face on the right side, taking in the eulogy.

Unfortunately, the man with the dark glasses did not recognize anyone but John Tannon and to John's right was an individual who looked like a cop of some kind. It must be the person blue eyes men-tioned. The sun-glassed man took a picture of everyone as he did in Paris a short time ago. Well, at least he didn't have Raines to worry about, as that would be the last thing he wanted; the man was scary. He went on to tell her of another plan that could make someone quite insecure using explicit pictures he took in Paris.

"So, let's get out of the city for a bit; we should be back this eve-ning. We have a job to do. It will be fun, the sun-glassed man said maniacally.

"Will we be killing anyone today or just making someone's life miserable?" she asked.

"Naw, this is a day trip to a small town called Westport; it's in Connecticut."

CHAPTER 18:

DOWNTIME;
WELL, SORT OF

After spending a few vacation days in Paris upon completing the protective detail, Cameron and Sara thought it might be good to head home. However, before leaving the hotel and being driven to the airport by Chief Brun, the chief had a few words to say to Sara. He scolded her first by saying, you promised not to get in trouble, but you did anyway. Chief Brun had a deep voice, so his words sounded intimidating, to be sure.

Finally, the chief told everyone to sit down as he had something else to say. "Sara, twice on the operation you were involved in, and twice you saved our necks and a couple of good men in the van. We thank you."

"Bien que je ne cautionne pas vos mouvements ici à Paris, nous, y compris Cameron et Yates, apprécions ce que vous avez fait".

(Although I do not condone your movements here in Paris, we, including Cameron and Yates, appreciate what you did.)

Sara did not know what to say. She just reached out and hugged him. Cameron gave the chief a big handshake and thanked him for the assistance.

So, the chief got Yates on a plane and told him to stop by whenever he was in the area. Yates says he would. As for Cam, the chief said that he is a lucky man to have Sara and vice-versa.

Before departing, Yates turned and told Cam that whenever he had an assignment that he needed help with, he shouldn't hesitate to call and bring Sara; she's prettier.

On the plane ride home, Sara asked Cameron, "You speak French, don't you? Why didn't you tell me after all these years?"

"To be honest, you keep telling people that I don't speak French; then, you only gave me a partial statement of what was said. It wasn't until you showed me what you could do in the MMA ring and the journey here to Paris that I have now understood who I fell in love with. So, I guess we are even?" Cam said with a smile.

Sara's eyes filled up with tears. Then she punched him kiddingly in the arm. "We're even, now!"

A few moments later, Sara staring straight ahead, said, "Cam, there is something else I want to tell you. We are…" then she turned and looked at Cam; he was fast asleep. Perhaps another time soon, she thought.

They landed in Boston, retrieved the car, got their package from customs, and then got a rapid test for covid, which seemed to be the norm in the travel world nowadays. On the way home, Sara asked Cam if all the jobs were like this; his reply had been a shrug of sorts as he was very preoccupied with thoughts about the whole Paris job and what they could have done better to prepare and what they could have avoided. While, of course, most of them did not have the terrorist side to them, they operated as though they all did. But then, an alarm chimed from his house via his phone; hopefully, it was a false alarm. Strong winds or a branch off a tree could be several things that could be the cause of it.

Driving with light traffic for about one hundred and sixty-two miles took almost 3 hours. Another twenty minutes or so to get home. Sara had slept most of the way, with her hand entwined with Cam's. He was looking forward to some downtime. That said, a protective detail could pop up anytime.

He woke Sara, and she had said, "Did I sleep long?"

"From the time we got out of Boston, otherwise not long, ha-ha." Cam laughed out loud.

He drove up the driveway and had one of those funny feelings.

"Sara, stay in the car; something does not feel right." Cam headed towards the front door.

Cam searched for any suspicious activity or anything out of the ordinary or a front door breach, but no signs. He checked his phone, and it indicated security issues on the door on the backside of the house. He cautiously went around the rear, found a couple of knives that he had hidden in the shingles of his house, and tucked them in his belt. The yard looked normal with all their ninja-type courses in place, but Cam found the back door slightly altered. A very subtle sign. So, it wasn't the strong winds or a tree branch. It seemed like a professional of some kind had done this. Although, to the naked eye, it didn't look like anything was amiss. His phone indicated this was the only breach. He texted Sara in the car and told her to stay there. Upon entering the house, nothing seemed out of place on the first scan, and then he spotted something on the kitchen counter. Pictures. Pictures of him and Yates in Paris specific to the operation, including the back alley at the convention center and the airport, and both jets before takeoff.

The pictures had a note attached. "I know who you are, and if I were you, I would watch your back, always. So, my best advice is to stay out of our way, final warning."

CHAPTER 19

TERRORIST PLOT

In New York City, blue eyes took out her contacts and rubbed her eyes. She then removed her wig as there was no need for a disguise at this time. Honestly, she thought who would be looking for me in New York City, as she was recently in Russia. They were laying low for a while and refining their plan to take down as many significant landmarks in NYC as possible. This terrorist event would more than rival the terrorism act in the mid-'90s, which included tunnels, government buildings, and the Washington Bridge, which failed.

Her partner thought there was a lot to plan, get it right and be out of the city when it all went down. It would be one landmark after another. So he went downtown to an abandoned building that he had just purchased which had many storage bins on one side, some stored with legit items. Still, many had explosives disguised as everyday items such as furniture and the like, which he would be putting in moving vans. Blue eyes knew her partner had been working on this for quite some time.

The plan was to load the trucks with as much of explosive materials, make them look legit, stage the loads in different directions, and detonate them at staggered times. The hope was that the blasts would create a crater at much as ten feet deep and at least fifty yards wide that could cause severe damage to infrastructure that years of reparation could not restore.

The other more pressing issue was eliminating all possible persons that could get in the way. Of course, this part of the plan had to be completed sooner rather than later. But, again, time and planning were on his side.

He was sure that the trip to Connecticut got Cameron Stones' attention and angered him, so predictably, he would very likely show himself and make mistakes.

His female partner in crime was very comfortable putting lots of explosives together with no regard for human life and mixing it up one on one or with whoever wanted to fight. But, as things progressed, he would have to keep her on a tight rope; she was a sick woman and unpredictable. As the weeks went by, the plan became more of a reality, but they first needed to eliminate anyone who could get in the way of their operation.

CHAPTER 20

THE INVISIBLE MAN

Raines knew the most noteworthy thing about being dead was that you can pretty much go anywhere with the proper disguise. No one would be looking for you.

John Tannon showed up, and Raines had him sit down for a serious conversation.

"So, John, who resided here before I made you the owner? And who made all the great revisions to the armament of the house, its armor is imposing?"

Tannon answered that he put in the bulletproof windows and re-enforced the walls, but as for the basement, "I thought you may have done that years ago, so I kept it clean when you called and got me back on board. Is there a problem? As to whom was here before, I never saw the occupant; everything was over the phone."

Raines answered, "Whoever made the changes planned something big and had added to the safe room an exit plan in case of retaliation or discovery."

Then, Raines got one of the phones that Tosh just happened to find. He had recorded the voice on the phone when he had picked it up the other day. But, unfortunately, the recording "Who's this?" was all he got.

"John, does this voice sound familiar?" Raines asked.

"Yes," said John. "That seems to be the same voice of the person I was talking with concerning this place. It's not a burner phone. They probably will shut off the service shortly, but we can see who this belongs to as Glover's people came and retrieved the men tied up a few houses down."

Thinking how in the world could that little guy, Tosh, surprise them, then zip-tie and secure them for the police, the police did not question Tosh's methods. "So, if we can pressure Glover to get these guys to open up a little, maybe we can get a name." added John.

"Sounds great," Raines agreed.

Tannon took Raines into the city, where Raines was getting a feel for the city's pulse like he had so many years ago. It hadn't changed much except there was not a lot of pedestrian traffic, mainly because of the Covid virus. All in all, the city seemed quiet. Too quiet, thought Raines, but that's when things happen. Horrible things. It was the calm before the storm that often left behind a damage so bad that even generations could not fix.

Raines's phone chimed; it was Detective Glover. That didn't take long. "Good afternoon, Detective; what can I do for you, and did you find something we could use?"

"Yes, a strong possibility. We have a hit," Glover paused for a second and asked Raines, "Do you know of a security, special ops guy named Mike Evans? He's been a person of interest of ours for some time. The voice recording you gave us was a ninety-five percent match. We ran it many times to be as accurate as we were going to be. When was the last time you talked with him?"

Although Raines had his suspicions about Evans, he could not believe what the detective said, not that he doubted him. "Yes, I spoke with him a few years back, always outside of extremist training camps of some kind. He said he was on a covert mission, keeping track of them. And he gave me some low-level protective details before I left the country."

"I don't believe he thought you would ever come back. We have also linked him to an attack in Paris involving a huge convention a short time ago in which he was not successful, and professional security teams shut him down. The city's security cameras showed him using some sophisticated tools in the area, but I feel it was just the tip of the iceberg. We believe he is very well funded and armed, but not sure by who. So perhaps that's the motivation; money. And Raines, now that we are connecting the dots, we feel he has a link to Lash Galik."

Raines's heart skipped a beat. Now it makes sense. Raines thought back to when he called Evans while in Australia a woman was screaming orders, and then the phone went dead.

"Glover, who was the detail leader in Paris for the convention, you wouldn't happen to know, would you?"

Just a few minutes ago, my colleague here gave me that information. The detail leader or one of them was Yates, does that ring a bell.

"Indeed, it does; no wonder Mike was not successful as Yates is a very serious participant in Close Protection, a term we have both used over the years. I'm surprised Mike escaped. You said one of them. Were there two detail leaders?"

"Yes, an American essentially headed up the detail. Would you like his name? So, Yates just had more experience in Paris and was well known by the police chief. And apparently, Mike had quite the loud diversion for his escape. One of the security vehicles was blown up, with personnel inside." Glover went on to say, "Let's assume that Galik is with him, she's very twisted, and he is one organized individual. He plans for all contingencies."

"And answering your other question, his name is Cameron, Cameron Stone," Glover added.

Raines thought that this was a lot of information to digest in a short period. John Tannon heard Raines's end of the conversation, and it would be all hands-on deck when it went down. Police often do not like it when private sector security gets involved. Still, in some cases, their perception of law enforcement training is a stark difference from the depth and experience of private security contractors. It is reactive versus proactive. They may need as much raw street-like intelligence and boots on the ground as possible if an imminent full-blown disaster happens in the city.

Tannon and Raines drove back to the house, both in deep thought, their location not all that far away. They both agreed they would need a place to stay in the city; their situational instincts would be at the forefront until then. But, in Raines's mind, it was a real disappointment that Evans, who he had known as a friend in a past life, would betray him and be a turncoat all for the almighty dollar. Eliminating him and his girlfriend would have to be the only way; keeping them alive would only allow them to find another way to escape again and be a threat to the society. But, on the other hand, Raines knew that he would sleep better at night, knowing that Galik would no longer haunt him in his dreams.

Glover spoke up and told Raines that they did some digging and came up with some intel to explain why Mike Evans had gone to the other side and the "why" he was at all these training camps. Raines pulled up a chair and said, "Go on."

"In 1999, Mike's parents were in Sudan on a humanitarian program when the U.S. attacked a factory believed to have materials for chemical warfare and weapons. No evidence supported whether there was or was not the intelligence to support this. News later came out that a pharmaceutical company had been bombed that provided medicine to its population. As a result, the medication for Malaria, Cholera, T.B., and a host of other treatable diseases was ninety percent destroyed, affecting thousands of people. Mike's parents were not among the small number of initial casualties but were shocked and stunned to the core that something like this would happen. Our intelligence shows that they either returned home or laid low for a couple of years, although they did a few interviews on radio stations abroad."

Raines was all ears as he listened to Glover give an enthralling recap, "The next time we heard about Mike's parents was 2001, most likely in October, the best we can put this together. Mike Evans's parents were on a philanthropical mission in Kabul, Afghanistan, working for the Red Cross. Mike escorted them there and thought it would be a great place based on their worldwide efforts. Plus, it seems he would be close by training. Unfortunately, there was a U.S.-led invasion that subsequently attacked the complex housing of the Red Cross in Kabul. Attacking and bombing a warehouse marked with the Red Cross emblem is a serious crime. There was another attack at the exact location a short time later, with food and supplies destroyed and civilian casualties. Although by the volume of the explosions, there was a munitions cache of all kinds beneath the common buildings at the site. Yet no one involved with the humanitarian effort wanted to believe that. Two of the losses were Mike's parents. Mike did not handle this well at all. We can gather that he went off on anyone who would listen. Mike threatened the government with lawsuits, personal attacks, and the like. The government even paid him substantial compensation for his losses and any therapy he may need."

"I'm sure he loved the money, as he was always that type of person," Raines added.

Glover paused for a minute, "For us here in intelligence, we had heard of an American going to bed with Al-Qaeda but could never get a lead on who it was until now. Through the years of investigating and concerning recent events, we now believe it was Evans who fed our agencies false information as to the whereabouts of Osama bin Laden. Our troops were running in circles and checking every cave in sight. These actions continued until we, meaning the government intelligence communities wised up and kept it more in-house. Finally, credible information had started in 2006 and continued to become more concrete that bin Laden was in Pakistan, and finally, as you know, Raines, we got him in 2011.

Glover then looked up at Raines, "Let me ask you a question if you don't mind. When did Mike come back into your life after you experienced your tragedy in 1991?"

Raines thought about it and said, "Around 2006, when we connected again, to get back in the fold."

Glover found it a coincidence that in 2006 he was in touch with Raines; the same year, we shut down most of the foreign Intel on bin Laden. Raines knew and had a good idea about what was going through Glover's mind and nodded his head.

"Well, in 1995," Glover went on, "there was a plan to blow up major landmarks in NYC, which was thwarted. So we think not only was Mike somehow involved with that but maybe thinking along the same lines currently if I haven't already mentioned that," Glover added. His psychological makeup now, based on his parents' death, has him going off on the deep end in the wrong way, while yours went completely the other way. Glad to have you on our side. His therapists, plural, owe me a favor and indicated he is a very sick man, a man bent on destruction and payback. I'm not sure that he even values his own life at this point. I want to add that the only person who seems somewhat more unbalanced than him would be Lash Galik. I don't think you would mind if she lives or dies at this point."

CHAPTER 21

WESTPORT TROUBLES / UNEXPECTED NEWS

Cameron checked the rest of the house for listening devices using the latest detection equipment. He found he had a lot of luck with the DefCon Security Products PRO-10G and went through the entire house. Sara had come in and sat on the sofa to watch Cameron do his thing. Next, he went to his monitor, which had video of the last twenty-four hours, hoping he had some footage of the person or persons who breached his house.

Finally, Cam spoke aloud, not knowing if Sara listened to him. "The break-in must have happened when we were in the air, as I would have had a notification on my phone of the breach. So, the whole break-in occurred within the last six or seven hours, relatively fresh."

The video footage showed two people, one male, and one female, walking around in the house. Both seemed to know where the cameras were as just profiles of each had been recorded. The party's male figure donned in dark sunglasses put a package of some kind on the counter.

A couple of hours later, Cameron deemed all was safe for conversation. Now, looking more closely at the videos, a call to the chief from Westport seemed fitting. The police chief seemed to have dropped everything he was doing and made it to Cam's house in record time.

Upon arrival, the chief began his serious questioning and looked at the pictures Cameron printed out from the recordings; he saw side profiles. A couple of images showed a bit more from another angle, but nothing conclusive. So, Cameron made some stock-ready copies for the chief and kept the first set. The police chief also looked at the images left behind by the mystery man.

"I have a feeling this man does not like you very much. What is it you do for work again?" the chief asked.

Cam answered like he always had that he was a security consultant for some big clients. Cam didn't divulge more than that; the chief didn't believe him but told Cameron he would follow up on the pictures and its note. The police chief would likely send the photos to a task force in NYC Hopefully, the images would not get lost with many other threats and pics that cross their desks. If the pictures were sent directly to them, then they would have time to do something about it and take some action before the threat was carried out or the tragic event took place.

The pictures made their rounds but fortuitously ended up in the NYPD Intelligence Bureau a couple of days later to analyze millions of faces with similarities to people in the database through facial recognition. This process would happen over a relatively short period.

Detective Glover walked in and kiddingly asked what the big deal on the screen was that everyone was waiting to look for. Just as he said that, the images stopped like it was on cue. On the screen larger than life was a person by the name of Mike Evans. Glover held his breath for a second and asked where they got the photos for comparison. Detective Williams, Glover's second in command in the

Intelligence Bureau, spoke up and said they got them from the chief in Westport, Connecticut.

Glover immediately got on the phone and asked the chief where these pictures came from. The police chief told the detective from a security consultant named Cameron Stone.

Meanwhile, Cam looked at Sara, and she seemed depressed in a way and asked her what the issue was other than these threatening notes and pictures. Sara looked up at him and said that there never seems to be the right time to tell you but here it goes.

"Remember some months ago when we shared an extraordinary, sparks flying, loving sexy moment well before you started heading out on the road again?" Cameron went to interrupt. Sara put her hand up and silenced him. "Well, as time has gone on, I haven't been feeling well. The excitement in Paris gave me a perfect reason to slow down a bit." Cameron thought sure it was a touch of the flu or perhaps Covid. "Ok," Sara continued, "You and I are going to have a baby."

Cameron did not see that coming but then hugged her, knowing he hadn't misunderstood her. And then, like many, said the infamous words, "How did that happen?" Sara had no comeback, but both smiled; a river of tears of happiness overwhelmed them. They were going to be parents, unexpectedly, but were over the moon at the news. Cam and Sara's relationship only blossomed since the day they met and even though the pregnancy was unplanned it was the right time in their relationship to take the next step.

Cameron's phone chimed, and the voice on the other end said, "Did you get my pictures from Paris that I left for you?" After a few hard expletives, Cameron regained his composure and said to Sara, I need to go out in the backyard to let off some steam.

CHAPTER 22

TEAMWORK

Detective Glover decided to visit Cameron Stone to ask him about the pictures, what had happened at his house, and related security issues. So, he called first, and Cameron answered, somewhat annoyed as he didn't recognize the number.

"Mr. Stone, this is Detective Glover from NYPD Intelligence. Will you be home this afternoon? I want to ask you some questions about the pictures you received from a video source some days ago. I received them to analyze and to confirm their identities. We can all work together on this issue as I have heard you can handle yourself quite well regarding serious situations." Glover seemed straightforward.

"Sure, come up. We can meet at a local eatery called the Spotted Horse Tavern. Great place," Cam went on.

Glover indicated that they would be talking about a person of interest they both had contact with, but not in a good way. That information piqued Cameron's curiosity. A couple of hours later, Detective Glover met Cameron at their agreed meeting place, with Sara sitting at a different table. Cameron motioned him over, asked to see his identification, and after Cameron was satisfied that Glover was indeed who he said he was, he said, "You first."

Glover had to tell him everything and indicated and confirmed through another source that Mike Evans was in many global areas where ISIS seemed to have been training for something huge.

Cameron gave the pictures to Glover, knowing that he had already seen them.

Glover nodded his head and said, "So, to the best of our facial identification experts, the man in the picture is Mike Evans, a Special ops guy who is and has been a mercenary for hire for quite some time." Glover thought for a minute and said, "We understand you had quite the security detail in Paris, you and Yates."

"Yes, we lost some good men both on the security end and in law enforcement. But unfortunately, we also let the bad guy get away," Cam added.

"The man is a known terrorist now and very good at what he does. However, now that we know he is in the city, we also need to look out for a woman named Lash Galik. They are together, and she may be under an assumed name and cloaked with a fake disguise and IDs to match. She is, by our standards, a very sick woman, but not from a health standpoint, if you catch my drift. She's well trained in all forms of hand-to-hand combat, and she also escaped capture a little while ago in a Russian republic. A nice couple in a twisted way," Glover added.

Cameron asked, "Is there anyone you know who has seen this person, Lash Galik?"

"Yes, Yates, who you are familiar with and another person. Trust comes in at this point," confided Glover, "So keep this to yourself. A guy named Raines would be very interested in her whereabouts."

"I hate to break this to you," Cam said, "But he died during an assignment in Australia a little while ago."

Glover smiled and said, "He is very much alive and in the hunting mode. He faked his death to continue searching for the person responsible for his family's death—a very skilled individual. Raines lost his family thirty years ago to a recently identified bomber/terrorist Lash Galik.

"Raines seems like a good man to get to know on many levels," thought Cam out loud.

Glover looked at Cameron and began his Intel about the information they piece-mealed through the years concerning Lash Galik. "Raines knows all I am about to tell you but wanted to bring you up to speed. Many years ago, we think mid-seventies, young Lash was kidnapped from her house, her parents were helpless to do anything, and they shot her father dead on the spot when he protested. Then, along with several other young girls and boys, they enslaved them. They were beaten, made to do manual labor, and the ones that showed promise to their captors were brought to camps to train. Most of these children were between ten and fifteen years old. Their captors would put them in a ring, one on one, like a dog fight at the training camps, and whoever won got an extra meal that day. Through our sources, we found that although Lash did not win every day, she did hold her own against older and larger opponents; she is a scrapper. Food was a great motivator for her; the more she trained, the more she won. Soon, they were betting on her. Her captors treated her very special, giving her what she needed to survive; the caveat was that she had to perform for them in the ring. Often they pitted her against some of the men in the group while she was still in her teens. She did exceptionally well for herself. Many in the group lost money because of her animal-like ferocity in the ring against all comers. They took her to the range, trained her in all kinds of martial arts, it seems, had her do the obstacle courses, and put her in the ocean far enough that it would be a challenge to get back for anyone. Yet, she excelled at all of it. There wasn't much that the men could do that Lash couldn't. However, she kept up incredible stamina and grit."

Glover took a deep breath and asked if he should continue. Cam nodded. "So here is where we lost her for a while. We only heard about a crazy woman involved with some piracy issues in the Gulf of Aden in the 1990s. Before the piracy, she was responsible for the 1991 bombing in NYC, where Raines was on that fateful evening. It looks like she works for the highest bidder. Then comes Mike Evans, birds of a feather."

"So, the real reason for meeting you was three-fold; one, to say that we are hunting the same party that escaped you in Paris; two, his partner is the same person who was instrumental in the bombing in nineteen ninety-one, and three, the picture of your girlfriend. She'll be in danger now. So here is the photo that our office intercepted, don't ask me how, but here it is."

Cameron looked at it, and it was a photo of a woman standing on the top of a building in Paris with long blonde hair. Cameron knew it was a photo of Sara just after she subdued the sniper. So, he waved her over to where they were sitting and showed her the picture. Her eyes shone green but not in a way he had experienced in the past.

"What do you need from us?" asked Sara.

Glover replied, "It's clear they know where you live. So, we can either move you to a safe house or have one or more of my people stationed around your home for you instead of a local LEO." Sara chose to have protection at her home as she knew every inch of it; plus, she said she hadn't been feeling that well.

"If you don't mind," Glover went on, "Cameron, I'd like to see your home, see the layout and then send the specs to the protection detail for your girlfriend's sake, although I heard a rumor that she is most likely better than anyone I can put on for cover and protection."

Cameron liked the idea of having Sara covered as he didn't mention to anyone that she was pregnant. It seemed like he was just getting used to the impression it made on people, namely himself. So, he will be a dad. Wow! Who would've thought?

Glover was thoroughly surprised at the fitness setup outside and in the house. "I take it you both work out a little. It seems like an understatement. I'd either like to take my team out here or personally watch the two of you work out. Very impressive." Even in the living room, some high bars were supported by the high ceiling. Then he said, "Ok, I will talk to the team, and Cameron, one day within the next few weeks or months, depending on our Intel, I would like you to meet the team working on our problem."

Cam asked, "Can you tell me what this problem might be?"

"We think there will be a massive terrorist attack soon similar to that which failed in the mid-nineties. We checked some cell conversations and investigated some abandoned buildings in or around mid-town. We are getting bits and pieces so far. We strongly believe Mike Evans, and even Lash Galik are the masterminds behind it all. No real confirmation on Galik, though. I will let you get settled a little before calling you back. We'll stay in touch. It sounds like the Paris project was intense, but in the end, you kept your client safe. Not sure how you and others do that work all the time but thank you."

About twelve weeks later, Cam received a call from Glover suggesting that it may be time to meet the team. He gave Cam the address to the house in the village where Raines, Tosh, Tannon, and Glover would be. Cam waited until the protection team arrived at his home before leaving. Sara had everything all tightened up. Their twelve weeks of not doing anything away from home allowed both of them to exercise as much as possible, with Sara taking it easy on some tumbling with leaps and flips off the roof.

Cam got to the house and knocked loudly; a slightly built Asian man answered the door and said, "May I help you?" with a Japanese accent. Then a much larger man walked over and said, "Come on in."

Glover introduced everyone in the room and finally said, "The big guy here is Raines."

Raines spoke first and said, "Heard a lot about you, your ethics and training in the close protection business and all from the private sector, very impressive. I also heard you had a run-in with my friend Mike in Paris. He's fast, well-armed, and very well trained, plus his girlfriend is a dangerously ill terrorist. We need to stop them."

Raines turned his head and said," Glover, you may want to cover your ears on this one, but there will be no mercy, or you have the right to remain silent comments unless they are dead." Cameron nodded in agreement. "Tonight, Tannon and I will be on surveillance regarding some abandoned properties to see what information surfaces. Perhaps once a week, we will be doing this and stagger the days and vehicles unless we find something. I will give you a call or Glover the next time we go out. We really would like to set a trap and have all the best people in place. No escapes this time. Any questions?"

Glover jumped in and added, "We can also send some stealth-like black drones out at night to see what the activity could be." While he purposely did not ask or answer any questions, Raines was right.

Raines laughed and asked, "What kind of drones? I've been out of the loop and just started getting better with electronics, so talk to me."

"So," Glover went on, "Drones of today are great surveillance tools in that we can spy on people of interest in a more covert way, mostly at night."

Cameron spoke up and said, "We will get them both; big favor though, I'd like to keep my girlfriend out of his. As much as she would like to be involved, she's very talented, but she is expecting."

Glover looked in his direction, somewhat surprised but realizing his team needed to step it up to keep an eye on her movements, as it was two lives now, not just one. Cam indicated that he would be available when needed but typically about an hour away. Right now, he thought he would head home and spend some time with Sara as he realized it could be a hectic and potentially deadly season.

Cameron took his time getting home as it was late, not a cloud in the sky, and he'd been gone all day; it would be good to be with Sara and her growing baby bump.

After about an hour of driving, he was close to home when he noticed emergency vehicle lights very close to his house. The closer he got, the more evident it became that it was his house.

Police vehicles, ambulances, and emergency rescue were all over his home. Yet, the only thing he cared about was Sara. He ran to the first ambulance, was questioned by police, and saw two officers lying side by side. Cam couldn't tell if they were out or dead, blood all over the place.

He looked up and saw the paramedics taking Sara out of the house, her face beaten and a hole in her shoulder. Cam screamed. Sara opened her eyes and said, "Get that bitch," and she lapsed into unconsciousness.

The paramedics looked at Cameron and said, "Where should we bring her? We have her stable with fluids and nutrients right now, and it does look like the baby has a good heartbeat, and that's a good sign."

Cameron asked if it would be too far to drive her to Mount Sinai Hospital and Medical Center in the City? They gave Cam the directions on his phone as if he was currently going anywhere but the hospital. The paramedics kept her stable and monitored the baby's strong heart rate. While following the ambulance, Cameron called Detective Glover and told him of the bad news that his officers may not make it. Cameron relayed that Sara used "Get that bitch" before passing out. So, Cameron surmised it was a female attacker. Glover relayed the info to Raines as it might be the person he had been hunting for all these years.

Cameron knew that Sara was in good hands and immediately headed to the fortified house in the village just outside the city. He was shocked upon arrival; the house was engulfed in flames. The fire department was there and had the fire about fifty percent contained. Cameron got one of the fireman's attention and asked if anyone was in the house when the fire started. The answer was negative as far as they knew.

Cameron dialed Glover's number, and the detective answered it. Cameron gave details of what he witnessed and asked if everyone was ok. Glover swore aloud but told Cameron of their position and immediate action plan. Glover went on to tell Cam that they are holed up in an old building, most likely scheduled for demolition soon. It looks like a construction site complete with chem toilets and modern amenities. A few homeless people were walking around but not paying attention to anything in particular. The target site is located opposite the street and down a few buildings from their position. He indicated that Cameron should park about two blocks away and hurry as the potential for stopping terrorists may be moments out.

CHAPTER 23

"MICHAEL"

A massive explosion rocked New York City in nineteen ninety-one, almost leveling the Regency Hotel. The blast's concussion ripped a small boy from the hands of his mother and flung him like a rag doll across the street. He hit a tree, before he crumpled to the ground and disappeared into the pile of rubble. The small boy, covered with dust and debris, was overlooked by many bystanders as the panic had people looking out for themselves and their own families. An older gentleman had arrived after the initial blast to see if he could help anyone, and it was pure luck that Roger Stone while watching where he was walking, looked down and saw a small arm. He gently cleared the wreckage and discovered a small boy who, much to his surprise, was still alive. Roger ripped part of his shirt off and applied it to the child's face with no time to call 911; Roger put the young boy in his car and drove him to Mount Sinai Hospital.

Roger knew that he would get the best of care there. They quickly moved him into the emergency room and cleaned him up, discovering that his face was missing half of its skin. Most likely, the young child suffered a concussion as well. Roger called his wife Margaret, and she arrived at the hospital. After a few days, the boy had awoken and screamed. The doctors gave him a sedative and pain reliever. They scheduled surgery on skin graphs and facial reconstruction. With plenty of TLC from everyone, the young boy stirred. As he opened just one eye, for now, the team asked him the most important question, "Do you know what your name is?" The young boy stared back with a blank look on his face.

Roger and Margaret Stone treated him with tender care as the weeks turned into months. The bandages removed over time indicated that the skin grafts worked well. The scar was hideous to look at, but as the doctors told them, it would heal in time, not entirely disappear, but he should look much better in a couple of years because of his age. The Stones observed the young boy smiling from ear to ear whenever their son Cameron entered the room. They were the same age and size, with similar interests as eight-year-olds. The Stones didn't want the child to go into a foster home. So instead, they kept him and named him Josh. They lived, in a medium-sized house, nothing fancy but comfortable. Overall, they didn't hear anything about a missing child or any child amongst all the rubble the explosion left behind some time ago.

Cameron looked after his brother as kids do; the locals made fun of him and teased him about his scar, but Cameron protected him. That said, many times, Josh waved Cameron off and defended himself. While not always successful, Josh felt the need to protect himself.

As the years went by, both children excelled in all subjects. Margaret and Roger were proud of both of their sons. With Josh, they had to apply for a birth certificate and other legal documents to make him their legal son. They had some contacts who respected what the Stones were doing and saw Josh's love for his parents.

The closer they got to their eighteenth birthdays, the boys figured out where they may want to go to college to start the rest of their lives. While both parents made suggestions, they left it to their boys where they wanted to go and what they expected to accomplish in life. Cameron somehow came across an ad about close protection work and delved into it with a lot of passion. While Josh thought that being in the medical field and helping people would be a great way to go. So, they looked for the best medical school for him. Funds were not an issue. For Josh, it was The Medical School at Harvard University. Roger was secretly praying that Cameron would do something similar; instead, he studied all he could about terrorist activities, and his physical training would eventually become obsessive.

As the years went by, both Cameron and Josh became very gifted in their respective fields. Then, one night a short time after their twenty-eight birthdays, Josh woke up from what seemed like a bad dream. He yelled and sat straight up in bed. Roger had come in first and asked him what the matter was. Josh relived the explosion some twenty years ago.

"Dad," Josh asked, "My real name isn't Josh. Is my name Michael?"

Roger and Margaret knew this day might one day come. Thankfully Josh was older now and could perhaps handle what happened.

Roger cleared his throat and said, "Josh, we found you in a pile of debris. You were almost dead; by luck, I saw your small arm and rushed you to the hospital; otherwise, you would not have made it. We knew that we could provide the care you needed to get well and grow into the great young man you have become, and you have a brother Cameron to watch out for you. So, you say your name is Michael; then Michael, it will be. Lots of identification to change, but we can do it."

Josh looked at him with tears in his eyes and said, Dad, my name is Josh now; you saved my life. Can I ask you what happened to my parents? The only thing I can remember is being with my mother."

"Your mother did not make it," Roger replied, "And your father was reported missing or has passed as well. I'm sorry."

"One more question, what was my father's name, do you know?"

Margaret entered the room, heard the question, and said, "We need to tell him."

Roger held Josh's hand and said, "Some years ago, we were curious about that very question. We had inquired in length with different departments and came up with one name. Your father's name is Edmund Raines.

CHAPTER 24

EVIL TIMES THIS WAY COMES

Lash returned to the abandoned house in the city where she hoped to meet with Mike Evans. But unfortunately, he was in a fortified office.

Lash spoke first, "I took care of the blonde you mentioned in Paris. She is quite a fighter and quite an athlete. She was swinging from an apparatus coming down from the ceiling and throwing kicks and punches upon landing. Never had a woman or man fought me like this before. Very accomplished.

Mike was intently scanning monitors of camera activity strategically placed for three-hundred-sixty-degree viewing. He did not seem to hear her enter through a series of locks and scans, nor did he look like he cared.

Mike asked Lash, "Sounds like you were impressed. Did you kill her?" Still concentrating on the monitors.

"As our fight began, she must have hit an emergency button somehow in the middle of our scuffle as I was lucky and left seconds before the police had shown up. Although she tagged me quite well,"

Mike looked up to see one eye closed and swelling around the other, "I managed to mess up one of her legs and..."

"She did all this while being pregnant, quite the amazing woman, so did you kill her?" Mike asked again.

"As I heard the sirens, I shot her but did not have time to check whether she was dead or not. However, I did put to death the police officers there to offer protection." Lash held her head low, looking for acknowledgment that she did well.

Mike explained, "At the very least, she will not be one we will have to deal with, just her boyfriend, and he has a mysterious partner of which I need more Intel. In addition, we now own six vans full of disguised explosives, so it changes the timetable to a few days from a week. We also know we are under surveillance. So, I may send an empty van out to see what might happen." He was going to do this sooner than later.

Mike continued, "If it comes down to a firefight or whatever it may turn into, save yourself. We have a team of well-versed and well-trained mercenaries who get paid big bucks to ensure our success. However, if you opt to engage, I can't help you unless we are together, am I clear?" Mike thought about the team meeting and how to get everyone in one place at one time. But, unfortunately, and hopefully, this would not be the place, or so he thought.

Lash nodded her head, but Mike could almost see a sadistic smile on her lips.

Mike started to make the phone calls to a dozen-plus evil characters, the kind that even he would not like to meet one on one. They would meet at an abandoned warehouse about a mile away. He scheduled the meeting with everyone and left his building through one of the escape holes he had made, and then he could blend into the night without being seen. Mike told Lash to stay put.

When the empty van left the house with an oversized garage attached, Mike slipped out the side door to a hole in the fence to another place using trees as cover until he was about six houses away. He then hailed a cab in which one of his men was driving and went down the street, took a series of lefts and rights, then doubled back to get to the warehouse. All these moves gave him an idea of whether he was surveilled or not. Finally, Mike walked into the warehouse and saw the most formidable group of fifteen hardened hand-picked men he had ever seen. Mike went into the plan and expectations. When he finished, no one seemed to have any questions. Mike needed six drivers that weren't afraid of getting their hands dirty; little did they know it was a suicide mission for those who volunteered. The rest needed to exercise their physical skill sets, including killing the so-called good guys who may get in their way. Most had hands raised for both jobs. There were slaps on the back and a lot of boasting of what they could do.

One of them spoke up and asked, "So, just curious, who is it that we are supposed to break?"

"Well, we know that NYPD intelligence is involved, a detective named Glover. We also know about a private sector security guy named Tannon and Cameron Stone, who I met in Paris. Cameron's mind will be preoccupied, as another associate of mine messed up his expecting girlfriend. However, do not underestimate Cameron; he is very good at his tradecraft.

The group laughed, and each spoke in unison. "So, does it look like we are worried?"

Evans shook his head, "Now's not the time to be overconfident."

CHAPTER 25

BATTLE PLANS

Glover, Raines, and Tannon monitored his drone's images and movements, and they saw the van leave. Glover's new drones were a distinctly altered version of the Holy Stone HS720 Foldable GPS Drone with a 4K UHD Camera and a long life with two batteries. They saw some action in the shadows, a heat signature, sliding from building to building in a human form. Glover thought it could be anyone and decided to track his movements and see what might develop. The figure got in a cab, drove around seemingly in a circle, and stopped at an abandoned warehouse about a mile away. Glover sent out another drone and directed the first one back to the team's hideout close to the first building for charging. Raines looked around and saw no signs of Tosh, not that he worried, just wondered where he was.

Tosh started nosing around the abandoned house after Glover indicated someone had left. There was a faint light inside. He also peeked inside the oversized garage and noticed five vans inside. If he could get inside, he could understand what was in the vans and their possible intent. He climbed up an outside power cord to get through a window only he was small enough to access. He lowered himself down into the garage, where he first scanned for cameras. Luckily or unluckily, he spotted two of them. Tosh stayed in the shadows the best he could and made himself a smaller than a human target, should anyone be watching.

The garage door began to open without notice, and in came the van that previously had departed earlier in the evening. Tosh stayed where he was for the time being. He talked silently into his radio and indicated to Raines and company where he was and that the previously departed driver had come back. They squelched twice on the radio to mean they received and understood.

Tosh slithered his way between the vehicles peeking in the rear of each of them. The doors unlocked on most of them. He entered the farthest one from the cameras. Unfortunately, the light in the vehicle came on as soon as the door opened. Tosh disabled the light quickly but swore at himself for not thinking ahead.

Lash Galik was inside the secured room casually looking at the cameras and noted the empty van returning from its little mission. She also saw that the driver left the building as he did not have access to the operation room. So, chances were he would return to the rest of the party a mile or so away. Her eyes briefly left the cameras, but out of her prereferral vision, she saw a curious light came on in one of the vans. The light went off almost in an instant.

Tosh located what looked like a timer of sorts but not activated yet. He was very familiar with most of the designs, so he followed the wire, and he found it was connected curiously to furniture. Interestingly, he found the end plugged into the furniture objects and carefully disengaged the connection but left it in place. It wouldn't look like it had been disturbed to the casual observer. Tosh left the van out of the backside very quietly. Four more to go, he thought to himself just as the door opened to reveal a short woman with dark hair and silent as a cat, a feral one at that. She went one way; he went another, no sense tipping his hand.

She entered the van previously occupied by Tosh and found the overhead light smashed. Damn, she thought and immediately gave Mike Evans a call. She told Mike about what she saw and that they may have had a breach. Her apprehension was too close to the operational timeframe to be concerned about any hiccups in the plan. As she was talking to Mike, she saw the door to the garage open and then close as a slight figure departed.

"Mike, a small figure just left the building, not much larger than a child; it looks like we had a hitchhiker in the van." Lash breathed a sigh of relief.

Mike indicated that they would be coming over within minutes as they had come too far for any doubts. So, he reiterated for her not to leave her current position. Lash didn't like to be told what to do and left the site as a homeless woman, grocery cart and all. She went down the street picking up some usable trash, playing the part. Lash saw what appeared to be people inside of a dilapidated building and kept moving, crossing the road and heading back to the terrorist's temporary head-quarters. She had information to relay to Evans and felt pretty good about what she may uncover.

A short time later, the whole crew arrived at the backside of the abandoned house and entered the operations room. Lash was very impressed by the men that Mike had recruited and the physical size of the men. It was their size and the hardened look on their faces like they had been to hell and back. One of the men sneered at her and said, "What can she do to help us?" After a few more condescending remarks, Lash walked up to him and kicked him on the inside of the knee faster than the eye could track. The big man collapsed painfully, and he saw her staring down at him. The man on the floor looked up and saw Lash's eyes, black as midnight.

After Mike pulled her away, she said, "Anyone else?"

"No, Ma'am," the men said in unison.

"Ok," Mike started as he helped the big man off the floor, "We'll have to assume we may have been compromised somewhere along the way, and may I add, respect her." Then, pointing to Lash, "And each other, we will accomplish our objective. Any questions?"

"When do we get to take out the people who want to stop us?" asked the group's senior member.

"They most likely will show themselves sooner rather than later as they will want to prevent us from doing whatever our opposition thinks we might do. So, we have put the whole plan on a need-to-know basis; only two of us know the goal, and now I will give you all the specifics." Mike got their attention.

"As I said back at the warehouse, I will need six drivers to all go in different directions, six of you who know the city, the lay of the land. The other nine will be with Lash and me to make sure we keep the best people on this job occupied to cover every contingency plan they may have."

Meanwhile, Detective Glover determined they would have to act fast to keep the vans from leaving across the road and down a block and with their drones picking up all activity in the house. At the same time, they would need to go all out to battle the small army assembled. This evening was going to be quite stimulating. So, Glover put a team together to include his partner Williams on full alert, mostly SWAT / Tactical Response and some government types that were very good in Anti-terrorism activities. Some of these officers would be in addition to the small team Glover had next to him. This team now included Cameron Stone, who had just arrived with a score to settle with Mr. Evans.

Cameron brought the package he acquired in Paris. But, of course, one of them would need to be invisible. Cameron guessed it would be Raines. Quite impressive, he thought, perhaps an understatement as he had male admiration for Raines's imposing presence as he did when they first met.

Tosh just arrived from his trip to the house and reported that one van was empty and another was disabled. He also mentioned that he would have disabled all of them, but a small woman walked in, eyes dark as a black hole. She may have seen him leave but couldn't get a bead on who he was.

Raines looked at him and said one word, "Lash."

Glover made sure all their coms were working and spoke out loud, "Everyone ready?"

Cameron's phone buzzed in his pocket. He reached in and shut it off. Cameron needed to be free of distractions.

CHAPTER 26

MOUNT SINAI

Sara arrived at the hospital bandaged up, the bleeding stopped, it seemed as though things would be alright during the one-hour ride, but Sara's body was fighting now to stay alive. The baby seemed healthy as they kept fluids and nourishment going into the IV that entered Sara and then the baby. Medically all should be working. But instead, Sara seemed to be in shock. Something medically was not going well. A lot was happening in her body.

Josh Stone worked at this hospital, and much to his surprise, from what he gathered, his stepbrother Cameron's girlfriend Sara needed immediate medical attention. After a few tests, she had to undergo surgery immediately to save her life. She was expecting, and Josh needed to save both of their lives. So, Josh took charge and got the best doctors the hospital had, told them of the situation, and that they needed consent first before they did anything drastic or otherwise. Josh found her purse. Inside, he found her phone and the number of his brother Cameron. His hands, slightly shaking, dialed the number. He heard it ring twice and then disconnected. Not knowing what Cameron was involved with, he sent him a text from Sara's phone.

"Cameron, this is your brother Josh. I am with Sara at Mount Sinai Hospital and Medical Center. We need you here. She is not doing well."

CHAPTER 27

COLLISION COURSE

Mike Evans got his six qualified drivers, not telling them they would not return, and gathered up the other nine anxious killers whose fate may precede their comrades.

The first van turned left and was immediately and suddenly surrounded by law enforcement, including dogs and bomb squads. They yanked the driver out of the truck, frisked him, and threw him in a waiting police van.

The Tactical Response Team leader radioed Glover and told him they got the first truck, but it was empty. The second van turned right, then took a surprise left, thus avoiding the trap set by law enforcement. The chase was on. Two more trucks were let loose at a high rate of speed. Spikes strips on the road dramatically slowed them down, resulting in occupants in each van being apprehended, and the bomb squads took over.

Glover thought it was time to move. At the same time, Mike Evans had a similar idea, and his team split north and south. In addition, Mike Evans seemed to have a good idea of where Detective Glover and the team were. So, he sent six of his most hardened, experienced, and mean-looking men to Glover's alleged location. Mike, Lash, and company were going to circle the building and put Glover and company in a pincher situation if he was right.

"Here they come," whispered Glover.

Raines looked around from his hidden location. Where was Tosh? Meanwhile, Cameron stepped out in the open facing six monsters. Tosh was curled up against the wall, looking like a bundle of cloth. When they passed, he stood facing their backsides.

One of the monsters looked at Cameron and said, "Out of the way, little man, unless you want us to move you, I thought you'd be bigger."

Cameron said with a smile, "Well, I guess you will have to move me, and I think you have me confused with the character from the "Roadhouse" movie, but this is no movie; this is real life, so do what you need to do."

The big man, red in the face, rushed at Cameron like a wounded rhino in a grappling mode, all three hundred and ninety pounds of him. Cameron waited, then leaped up and over the charging beast, landed and back kicked him face-first into the building, and then kicked the next man full force in the jaw with a jumping front kick. He went down but not out. The first man recovered, and a blur of rags seemed to materialize out of nowhere with an outstretched hand in spear-handed technique, fingers first and buried deep within the attacker's throat. One down.

Cameron heard the command "Duck," and a gun had discharged as he ducked. The bullet hit the man in front of him with a round to his upper torso. The force knocked him on his butt, which only seemed to anger the attacker even more. He got up. The second man and the fourth came at Cameron, and Cameron executed a jumping ax kick aimed at the attacker's collar bone. Just as he connected, another round went off from Glover's gun the fourth attacker went down. Cameron's attacker seemed to have a problem with his right arm but remained standing. Tannon stepped out from the shadows and tried his best to hold his own. Unfortunately, his training was insufficient as attacker five swatted him as though he were a fly. Tannon bounced hard off the building's facade. Glover pulled him to safety with his gun raised.

Tosh went over to attacker six, tapped him on the leg, and politely said, "Excuse me." The hulk of the man turned and saw this little old grey whiskered man staring up at him and started laughing. Then, using his inner chi, Tosh executed a palm heel strike as hard as he could muster into the liver of this behemoth of a man. The man swatted Tosh aside, then collapsed. Although somewhat dizzy from the blow, Tosh flew through the air and landed on all fours like a cat. Another shot rang out, and a bullet hit Tannon in the chest. Although he had a vest on, the force still broke a few ribs and most likely punctured a lung.

There was a slight rumble beneath their feet, and then a significant explosion ripped through the night. The abandoned building that Mike Evans used as a hideout in his quest to blow up historical points in NYC was no more. Nor was any building close to ground zero. Glover received a call from Williams, who indicated that they set a charge and blew the last two vans in the building, and the number two van had surprised most NYPD and TRT officers because the bomb had previously been diffused. Vans three and four were being disarmed and dismantled from the inside out. He also told Glover they were heading in their direction as it seemed like they needed help from what Williams could see from his vantage point. Glover was listening but also busy finding cover and pulling Tannon to safety, not knowing if he was dead or not.

Cameron turned around to find himself face to face with Mike Evans about fifteen yards away. Again, he didn't hesitate and threw one of his knife darts in Evan's direction. This time, it struck him in the leg.

Evans swore out loud and let loose a round in Cameron's direction. Cameron got out of the line of fire but was immediately grabbed from behind by attacker five. He threw Cameron hard up against the building. Cameron felt the big man's hands suddenly lessen in their grip on him and drop. Ninja-like, Tosh had jumped up and given the assailant two cupped hands to the ears simultaneously, most likely rupturing his eardrums. Number five would be in a lot of pain for a while. Meanwhile, Cameron had pushed off the wall with his legs, and both he and number five went to the ground with Cameron on top, no longer held by a giant man.

Evans drew a bead on Cameron and pulled the trigger. In a millisecond, Tosh pushed Cameron out of the way. In doing so got rewarded with a bullet that traveled across his back. Evans fired again and again, and the bullets ricocheted off the buildings, striking one of his men.

In a nearby alley, Lash cornered Glover and glared at him. Then, she violently kicked the gun out of his hand, breaking Glover's wrist. Tosh recovered somewhat, albeit with a bloodied back and the other injuries sustained, looked at Lash, and said, "Pick on someone your own size," and smiled. She turned and then let loose a barrage of hand techniques so fast that all combatants stopped briefly, amazed. What was more impressive was that Tosh blocked or evaded all the blows, but you could tell that all this violence and physical abuse was taking its toll on his ninety-something-year-old frame.

While all this was going on, Cameron, joined by Williams and crew, gave the new big band of ugly, mean, war-hardened men a fight that none of them would forget. Some of the big uglies went down after being tasered only to get back up. Some pulled the wires out and laughed. Cameron's training, stick-work, and athleticism kicked in as he ran, kicked, punched, and jumped. He landed each time executing perfect techniques into and at these enormous individuals. It was like running through a human obstacle course. His martial methods were designed to hurt, maim, or kill the attackers if needed.

Meanwhile, Williams was having a shoot-out with Evans as well. Williams's teammates were busy trying to subdue some monsters on the street. Some officers successfully ganged up on one, and some were thrown around like rag dolls. Two sides of the busy street looked like a gang war gone extremely bad with no one party getting the upper hand. Several good people went down, including Williams.

Lash was advancing on Tosh, who was exhausted and slumped against the building. He looked like he was on his last breath. Then, out of nowhere, she was kicked in the head very hard. After recovering, she looked around, nobody within eyesight, although there was a brick close by on the ground. What the hell, she thought out loud. She looked at Tosh, and he seemed to be fading.

"I will make sure you never get up again, old man," Lash said in a possessed voice that would make horror stories come alive.

Just as Lash was about to strike, she was pulled up in the air and slammed face-first on the ground by an unknown force. Her hands were duct-taped behind her back. Her legs were zip-tied and duct-taped together with a big piece put over her mouth.

A deep voice close to her ear said, "You killed my family thirty years ago. I will determine your fate after I talk to your boyfriend." Raines stepped out from behind the invisibility shield that Cameron let him use and stepped into the middle of the street.

Meanwhile, Cameron picked up a six-foot-long piece of rebar, a quarter of an inch in diameter. He was squaring off with one of the new grizzly-sized opponents that arrived. Swinging the steel like a bo-staff, he caught the giant on the side of the leg. Unfortunately, the man had lifted his leg at the last minute, and it seemed to be more of a nuisance than anything. Cameron backed him up, dropped the bar, and leaped at the giant for an elbow strike. The bear of a man caught him in mid-leap and squeezed. Cameron was about to press his ridge-hand on the underside of the big man's nose, a pressure known as the Infraorbital nerve, when he heard a slight cough from Tosh. Tosh was right in the back of them and looked around for a weapon, found a match, and set the massive attacker's pants on fire. Oh, how that worked, seeing a man dance around to put the fire out. Tosh found this amusing. The giant released Cameron, and Cameron spun and back kicked the man in the knee and followed up with a flying knee to the jaw. The man stood there for a second and fell flat on his face. Gunfire erupted all around them from all sides. Cameron pulled Tosh to safety.

In the middle of the Street, Raines called out, "Mike Evans, we need to talk." Time stood still.

Mike looked in his direction and looked like he saw a ghost.

"Raines," he said in an unbelieving wavering voice, "I was at your funeral. I thought you were dead."

"Very much alive and hunting bad people. Your girlfriend will not see the light of day for a while." It was then Evans looked around, and she was nowhere in sight. So, Raines told Evans to put down his gun and then prepare to dance, which means they will go all out in a fight to the finish.

Evans put his gun down, cautiously walked towards Raines, and said, "Good luck Raines. I taught you everything you know. So, this fight will be very predictable. This fight will be my pleasure." Raines smiled. Little did Evans know the amount of training Raines had endured during his downtime.

They both got out of the middle of the street. Mike looked very confident as he walked toward Raines. He came at Raines with a fast flurry of punches. They were all so quick and powerful that they seemed to connect in a blur. Much to Evan's surprise, Raines smiled and easily evaded them. Then Raines executed a thrust kick to Evan's stomach, Evans turned slightly, and the blow was hard but glancing. Secretly Evans removed a knife from his belt and slashed at Raines with a hidden blade technique.

The blade caught Raines on the forehead, not enough to damage, but all head injuries bleed profusely and would blind him momentarily. Evans rushed in as Raines went by feeling and other senses; this is where his practice of echolocation paid off and hit Evans under the chin with a Muay Thai elbow strike then a brutal knee strike to his ribs. It knocked Evans back about ten feet. Evans grabbed a nearby two by four and swung it at Raines, who lifted his leg in a Muay Thai position and the two by four broke. Raines could tell that he may have broken a few ribs on his former friend or caused some internal injuries and was hoping for both just the way Evans had swung the board. Raines could tell there was substantial evidence of rib damage. Evans pulled out a backup weapon and fired at Raines, but at the same time, Cameron had a running start and performed a textbook flying side-kick, which put Mike Evans through some windows at the abandoned warehouse. Cameron went over to Raines, who had blood all over his face and head area. The bullet looked like it creased his skull a little. He is still alive, unconscious but alive, going to have one heck of a headache for a while when he woke up. It was then that Cameron had turned and saw an approaching Tactical Response Team dressed for action. Emergency vehicles, paramedics, and his partner Phil sling were with them. Phil helped them weed out the good guys from the bad and the most injured. The TRT team rounded up all the perceived bad guys and thoroughly cuffed them, at least those still alive and able to move. They also gently picked up Raines, who looked like he'd been through war, blood everywhere, much of it superficial. The crease in his skull was worrisome, and they were not sure how deep it was.

Phil was the first to talk, "Hey Cameron, looks like you needed some help. Who is the big guy on the ground?"

"That my friend is Raines. What took you so long?" Cam answered.

Cameron mentioned to one of the senior members of the team and said, "The ringleader is through that window, and his partner is behind the screen. They found Lash but nobody in the building. Evans had disappeared again.

Cameron sat exhausted against the building and reached down to his phone. He turned it on and curiously saw that he had a text.

"Cameron, this is your brother Josh. I am with Sara at Mount Sinai Hospital. We need you here. She is not doing well."

"Phil, do me a favor and ask the paramedics to take Tosh, Raines, Glover, Tannon, and Williams to the Mount Sinai Hospital. I will meet you there." There was a new sense of urgency in Cameron's voice. Cameron remembered and respected that Phil was the one who took a bullet for him at the movie premier not long ago.

"You heard the man. Get these people to the Mount Sinai Hospital ASAP," Phil commanded.

Cameron said to Phil, "While I am at the hospital making sure everything is alright, I need you to go deep into the city, ask our contacts on the street about anything that may concern us, and pay them if you need to." So, Cameron gave him a wad of money for the assignment.

Cameron arrived at the hospital and was informed that he could not see Sara since he was not related. However, one call to his brother Josh cleared that misunderstanding quite quickly.

Josh's statement for his brother Cam was, "Sara may die. We can take the baby now and are reasonably optimistic that the baby will survive and be healthy, but Sara may not make it either way."

Cam had to make a difficult decision about the baby's delivery and give the infant the necessary care he needed. So, he went with taking the baby and praying for Sara. Sara was barely holding on. Finally, the medical team gently removed the baby from Sara's body. The nurses took him away with optimism; he had five fingers and five toes and was breathing well. Strong vitals.

Sara's breathing was shallow. Cam held her hand as tears rolled down his face. Then, he whispered, "It's not time yet. Please hang on. I love you." He prayed.

Josh walked in and saw his brother, and it was the first time he'd ever seen his brother Cameron so moved with emotion. As much as he wanted to reach out to his brother and comfort him, it was best to let him have his time with Sara.

Cameron's phone vibrated.

CHAPTER 28

REUNION

Raines was wheeled in a few doors down from Sara, and no one was sure what kind of shape he was in with a head injury caused by a bullet. The doctors shaved his head, stitched the knife wound on his forehead, and then tended to his skull and the crease caused by the gunshot wound. They cleaned it out, not much to stitch at this time; they wrapped his head, had him on an IV morphine drip, and monitored his vitals, which were solid. Josh was appointed as his primary doctor and looked at his chart when he realized who the person was that he was looking to administer medical care. Mild shock, butterflies in the stomach.

While Cameron stayed with Sara, her condition hadn't improved, nor did it worsen. The doctors did find that the poison-laced bullet that passed through Sara's shoulder had just enough poison to give her an immediate near-fatal reaction. The doctors indicated that she would not have made it ten minutes if the slug had stayed in her body. Blood transfusions and monitoring of her vitals and organs gave them all hope.

Cameron decided to take a walk and go to Raines's room to see how he was doing. He arrived just as Raines opened his eyes.

Raines's first words were, "Did we win?"

Cameron filled him in on what transpired after he took a bullet to the skull and that Lash was arrested and would be incarcerated behind bars for the rest of her life. Cam also told Raines that all other members of the attacking team were also under arrest, at least the ones left standing. The other ones that did not make it had the right to remain silent. He went on to say that they lost a few good men. John Tannon and Williams did not make it once they arrived here, and your friend Tosh may not make it either. Glover took a beating but will be ok.

Raines then asked, "Mike Evans, did we get him?"

Cameron told Raines how he had side kicked him through some windows just as the gun went off, causing the bullet to crease his skull. So, after helping others and coming out on top of the battle, for the most part, during clean-up, Evans was nowhere to be found. The reaction team had a couple of search dogs, but the trail went dead on the backside of the building.

"We'll find him, trust me." Cameron went on to say.

As Cameron concluded his recap, a doctor with a slight facial scar from his forehead down the side of his face entered.

"Well, good afternoon, Mr. Raines; glad to see you, and hi Cameron, good that you are here as well. I have some news for you." Both Raines and Cameron could see Josh's hands shaking a little.

As he looked at Raines, he said, "I don't quite know how to say this, but I found out you are my father. Although my name tag declares my name as Josh, it's the only name I've known. So, my real name that you gave me is Michael."

Michael went on to tell his father about his life and the care that the Stone family provided him. Cameron was all ears as well. Michael told Raines that it wasn't until he was in his twenties that bits and pieces of that fateful day came together.

"We all looked for you, but the conclusion was that you had passed away. So recently I went to your funeral and saw your friends bury you next to mom. Detective Glover had already told me who my real dad was. And before I was assigned to you as my patient, the doctors and Cameron filled me in the best they could regarding the type of man you are and what you did for work. You helped save a city today, Dad. And Dad, this man here, Cameron, saved your life. He's my stepbrother, lots to catch up on."

Cameron did not know until now that Raines was Josh's Dad.

Cameron could only mouth the word, "Wow."

"Welcome home," Michael/Josh whispered.

Not a man who shows much emotion, Raines had tears running down his face and hugged Michael with a loving embrace. Then, finally, Raines spoke up and said, "Can you take me to Detective Glover's room, please."

As they arrived at Detective Glover's room and talked briefly to the detective, who seemed to be on the mend, Glover thanked Raines and Cameron for being there for New York City and its safety. Then, they went from Glover's room to Tosh's room, where they found a very fragile man holding on by a thread for his life. He had a weak heartbeat but was still alive.

Tosh opened his eyes and signaled to Raines. "We did well together." He coughed in pain. He whispered again, "My time is up. I will die a good death." With that, he closed his eyes. Raines closed his eyes, tears again streaming down his face. He felt he had lost a father figure he never had.

The close bond between them had been solid for many years. They wheeled Raines back to his room; the silence was thick. Michael stood off to the side and knew it would be quite some time for all parties to decipher everything that had gone on in each of their lives.

Cameron's phone was buzzing, and he looked down; it was his partner Phil.

"Yes, Phil, what's going on?'

"Well, apparently, your client from Paris is here in the city. What was his name, you told me, a Mr. J? Curiously, we looked at some camera footage on the backside of the building a couple of blocks down from where you kicked Mr. Evans through some windows. The footage showed a stretch limo pulling away. We followed the stretch, and one got out; another person seemingly stayed in the car as the first person leaned on it to say something to the person in the back seat and then to the driver. Then, as my contact informed me, the limo headed downtown to a medical center. I am outside a bar in an upscale hotel on the east side, and the main guy is sitting down with a couple of individuals having a drink. I will take a picture of him and his barmates in a minute."

A few minutes later, Cameron received the pictures of three individuals at the bar, one was Mr. J, and the other two were identified shortly after. One person was identified as Bernard Jarrar. Bernard took his mother's last name, Lana Jarrar, the former wife of Carlos the Jackal, the latter who is still serving time. The other one is Fusako Meiling Shigen, wanted in Japan. As Raines held up the picture of Mr. J, he realized Mr. J. was Mr. Jones, the person whose life he saved in Australia a little over a year ago.

Cameron then told Raines and Michael that he would like to check on Sara to see how she was doing.

CHAPTER 29

DEATH'S DOOR

On his way to Sara's room, Cameron's phone rang again. It was Phil. "Yes, Phil, any more news on anyone?"

Phil told him of his street contact, observing a man getting out of the limo looking quite banged up and in a lot of pain. He needed a wheelchair to get him into the building. He could not see his face.

Cameron then heard the hospital's announcement, "CODE BLUE, CODE BLUE room 1128. "Got to move," Cameron said with a very stern voice; "That's Sara's room!"

The hospital staff would not let Cameron in the room as he wasn't related and would likely get in the way. So instead, they let him view from an observation room. Cameron watched as the staff set the pads upon her bare chest and administered the shock from the AED. It was then Cameron realized that her heart had stopped beating; the monitor showed a straight line as they were trying to bring her back to life. What was happening didn't seem real, Cameron thought to himself. This couldn't happen to her. The doctors tried for almost an hour and then pulled the sheet over her body.

Cameron cried out so loud that the doctors could hear him through the glass separating them. But then, his mode changed dark, and he left like a predator on a hunting mission for revenge, but this act was not before calling one of his best agents to secure the hospital floor. He called Dan, a very accomplished Close Protection Specialist, who had a permit to carry in NYC if things went south. Dan was with Cameron in getting the celebrity to safety during the red-carpet detail, which seemed like months and months ago. Cameron, full of anguish, left on an emotion-charged mission.

In room 1128

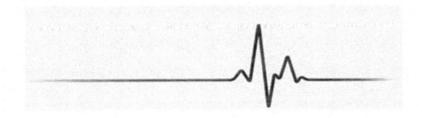